1777 SOCIETY

This book is a work of fiction. The names, characters, places, and incidents are products of the writer's imagination or have been used fictitiously and are not to be construed as real. Any resemblance to persons, living or dead, actual events, locales or organizations is entirely coincidental.

ONE NIGHT IN LONDON, 1777 Society, Book 1
© 2024 by Tamara Gill
Cover Art by Wicked Smart Designs
Editor Grace Bradley Editing, LLC

All rights reserved. Without limiting the rights under copyright reserved above, no part of this publication may be reproduced, stored in or introduced into a database and retrieval system or transmitted in any form or any means (electronic, mechanical, photocopying, recording or otherwise) without the prior written permission of both the owner of copyright and the above publishers.

ISBN: 978-1-923245-19-8 (trade paperback)

CHAPTER
ONE

1777, London

Lady Genevieve knew better than to sneak out of her father's London home in the middle of the night. Still, a friend in need came before reputation and sanctions, which her father would definitely impose should he ever find out about her escapades. Her mama would probably have a fit of the vapors and ask her long-suffering companion for smelling salts or her preferred much calming potion of laudanum.

Genevieve, whom she was known affectionately by her friends, used the ballroom doors that stepped out onto a large terrace overlooking their sizable gardens in the heart of Mayfair and tiptoed to the side of the house where she ran toward a gate hidden within a wall of ivy. Her voluptuous gown made working her way through the ivy difficult. She snagged a part of her dress on the gate and swallowed a curse. Why women had to wear such an absurd amount of material was a mystery she would never understand.

Male laughter and the sound of glass breaking seized her movement to a halt, and she waited in the ivy. Footsteps sounded on the pebbled road beyond, and then the undeniable voice of her brother, slurring his words of protest at having been sent home by his closest friend in the world, Beckett Green, Lord Tyndall, a vexing, teasing busybody of a man whom she had always secretly adored until he called her a carrot top and her infatuation came to an abrupt end.

How dare any gentleman—if he could call himself that—term a lady so. She had red hair, yes, and now, thanks to him, she went to great pains to hide it from society whenever possible. No one would ever know.

Nor would she ever let Lord Tyndall know of her childhood crush. His head did not need to become any more significant than it already was. Not to mention, she did not want several widows who sauntered the ballrooms of the *ton* to come after her with pitchforks. Not that they would, in truth, go after her with such weapons, but Lord Tyndall was a well-sought-after gentleman. He was titled, handsome, and wealthy. A matchmaking mama's dream, even her own.

But Lord Tyndall would never romantically look at her. He had often said over the years that she was too annoying and cloying and needed to go elsewhere and leave him and Martin alone to their manly business.

Not that she thought he had much men's business at sixteen, but ten years had passed since then, and he still looked upon her as if she were in pigtails and the annoying little flea who followed them around, begging to be included in their games.

But she did not need to be included any longer. She had two friends, the best of friends in the world, whom she would only ever need. Her brother could do what he liked these days, and it would be all the better if he stayed out of her way, for she had a husband to catch.

London's newest member. A gentleman from abroad, America, to be exact. He was handsome, rich, and the opposite of whom she had to dance with these past three years. But she was determined not to endure a fourth Season, hence why she was sneaking out with her friends to Lady Russel's ball, where Mr. Roger Venzellons was sure to be, and where she could continue her pursuit of him.

Rumor had it he enjoyed nothing more than the balls at Lady Russel's, and so that is where she and her friends were going, even if her parents forbade her and thought her in bed. What they did not know surely would not hurt. And Lady Russel's balls tended to be more demimonde rather than haute *ton*...

Genevieve pushed back into the ivy just when the nuisance Lord Tyndall decided the side gate was where he was going to bring her brother through. Unless she dived into the nearby roses, there was little she could do but be caught and seen.

She strolled the garden bed, leaning down to smell one of the roses just as her brother and Lord Tyndall stumbled through the gate. "Genevieve, is that you, sister?" Her brother hiccupped and chuckled, and Genevieve fought not to roll her eyes. "Either I'm more foxed than I thought, or my sister is gardening at midnight."

"You're not hallucinating, Martin. Your sister is indeed in the garden." The deep, annoyed timbre of Lord Tyndall's voice set Genevieve's hackles to rise, and she lifted her chin, no longer willing to be chastised by a man who was beneath her. After all, she was the daughter of a duke, and he was nothing but an earl. How dare he insinuate her being in the garden was anything other than her enjoying the roses at midnight? Plenty of ladies did so, she was sure, and she certainly would hold to that story and not let his lordship question her whereabouts. She owed nothing to him.

"Am I not allowed in my own yard, Lord Tyndall? Who are you to say anything about it?" she said, giving him her back and inspecting another rose that, at this time of night, she could not discern its color.

"Go in that direction, Martin, and you shall find the ballroom doors on the terrace. Find your room and sleep off your whisky," Lord Tyndall said, giving her brother a friendly push in the direction of the terrace. Thankfully, her brother did as he was asked and stumbled off until the terrace doors slammed closed, and her sibling was at least safe for one more night.

If Genevieve thought her interaction with the earl was over, she was sorely mistaken. An annoyed sigh sounded behind her. She rounded on him, hands on hips, and glared, even though she knew her face was in shadow due to the moon being behind her. "Why, may I ask, are you still here, Lord Tyndall? Should you not leave now that you've sorted my brother like an errant child?" Genevieve couldn't help but speak to his high-handed lordship in a scathing tone. The man was maddening, and she had never quite gotten over the fact that at the tender age of fifteen, she had thrown herself at his head in a fit of expectation and hope and had been sorely rejected.

Lord Tyndall had held her at bay with his hand on her forehead and laughed excessively in her face. She had never quite gotten over the embarrassment, and he damn well knew it. She could no longer remember why she had thought he was open to her advances. Perhaps he had smiled at her through dinner that evening or listened to her piano playing eagerly. They had been having a lovely holiday at her parents' ducal estate in Kent, and Lord Tyndall was there. Like always, he was always there, never anywhere else. More the pity. Especially the one where she had made such a fool of herself...

And here he was again, in her garden, chastising her. "A better question to be answered is why you're lurking in the gardens past midnight. I know from your brother that your parents were staying in with you this evening, which means you were also. So, would you care to enlighten me as to why you're outside smelling the roses quite literally?"

She narrowed her eyes, hating that even

while Lord Tyndall was insinuating a situation that was none of his business, whether it was true or not, he still was one of the most handsome men in London, with his shoulder-length hair that always looked perfectly coifed. The soft curls seemed to sit on his ideally proportioned head perfectly and made many a lady, herself included, ogle him from time to time. Not that she would ever admit to ogling him at all. Her infatuation had come and most definitely gone.

Mostly.

"I wanted to go for a walk, if you must know. Are you going to send me off to my room like a naughty child also?"

He watched her, silent and considering. Something in his dark gaze made her stomach clench. She swallowed and considered that perhaps he would indeed spank her like a child and send her on her way, and the idea was not without merit or intrigue. Would she like it?

Genevieve shook her head and the absurd thought from her mind and remembered her annoyance with his lordship.

"No, of course not, but I will not leave until you're back inside and safe. We will discuss your nightly pursuits another time, but now, I shall not budge until you're indoors where you belong."

Genevieve knew there was no use arguing with him. He was as bossy as her brother and just as high-handed, and she needed to sneak out again, perhaps not this night, but another and soon, and she did not need him lurking about ensuring she did not. Genevieve turned on her heel and started back toward the terrace.

"Goodnight, Lady Genevieve," his deep baritone said from behind.

A shiver ran down her spine, and she fought not to physically react to his voice.

"Goodnight, Lord Tyndall," she returned in a much harsher, cutting tone that her friends would be proud of, should they have heard it.

CHAPTER
TWO

Later that evening, Beckett sat in a leather wingback chair at Whites, idly sipping his brandy and staring onto St James Street. He tapped a finger against the crystal tumbler, thinking of Lady Genevieve and where she could have been possibly going this evening when their paths had crossed. Quite a serendipity, in fact, since she was obviously sneaking out somewhere in the dead of night, but the question was to where and to whom?

Were her parents aware of her nightly pursuits? A woman such as herself, an heiress with the face of an angel—as much as she acted like the opposite with that fiery red hair—should not be walking the streets of Mayfair at that hour of the night. She was courting trouble, and he would never forgive himself if anything happened to her, not now that he was aware of what she was up to.

He would have to speak to Martin about his suspicions and get him to forward the information to her parents to keep her safe.

Beckett took another sip of brandy, and the smooth texture of the beverage went down well after a night of revelry with his best and oldest friend, Martin. He could not remember a summer or London Season that did not involve the Duke of Curzon's family. His family, too, if truth be told. The only one he knew and loved. Lady Genevieve the exception. The termagant was a thorn in his side for the past fifteen years. Ever since she threw herself at his head that long-ago summer, their relationship had never been quite the same.

And he could understand why. She had embarrassed herself, and he had laughed at her immature infatuation with him.

But now... Well, now she was a woman enjoying her third Season in London. A beautiful, voluptuous woman whom many men had wanted to marry. And several had, in fact, proposed to Genevieve, and yet she denied them all. She had turned up that pretty little nose and politely said, *I do not* instead of *I do*. Not that Beckett could blame her. Her romantic heart yearned for love, and if she gave some of the gentlemen a little more attention, perhaps she could find that elusive emotion sparking between herself and another, but she did not. She was too busy with her friends, Lady Charlotte and Lady Matilda. Three eligible women who seemed determined to remain spinsters forever.

But then, mayhap not.

Where was Genevieve going this evening in one of her finest gowns? Not that Beckett took much heed of what she wore, but she was up to something, and he was determined to find out what that was before she found herself in trouble.

A ruckus sounded near the entrance to the drawing room, and Beckett turned. Mr. Roger Venzellons sauntered in with his merry band of fellow Americans. The man made Beckett's eye twitch and he followed their progression across the room to the bar where they stood and ordered an obscene number of drinks from the footman.

The leather chair across from his squeaked as Lord Wolfson joined him, glancing toward the bar. Beckett sipped his brandy and returned his attention to his present company, which was far superior to Roger Venzellons.

"I heard Mr. Venzellons is after a wealthy

English bride to take back to New York," Wolfson interjected. "He's built a grand place in Manhattan and requires more chattel to decorate it. Do you think he has anyone in mind?" Wolfson finished, lighting a cheroot.

"I figured when he and his posse arrived at the beginning of the Season they were after brides. I have yet to discern any great interest in the Season's debutantes. Only those of the married, unsatisfied kind of ladies are taking up their time, but what do I know? I'm not in their sphere of friends, so I'm happy to be proven wrong."

"Ah, well, you're not wrong. I was at Lady Russel's ball earlier this evening, and he was there, but his interest may lie in a direction that may shock you."

Beckett studied Wolfson, who clearly debated telling him this tidbit of information. "Well, will you not disclose what you have learned?"

"I can tell you all, but you must promise not to react. Not in any way. Take the information that I'm going to give you and be calm with it. Do you promise me that?"

Beckett narrowed his eyes, and Wolfson schooled his features. A sinking feeling that he would not like what he heard settled in his gut.

"Very well, I promise not to react to this news. Now get along with it and tell me." His patience waned, and he ground his teeth, never having much patience.

"Surprisingly, at the Russel ball, Lady Charlotte and Lady Matilda were there, but no Lady Genevieve, which I thought odd, considering the three of them rarely do anything alone. They're like a circle of friends as solid as a wheel. But Lady Genevieve was not there, and that was how I came across another bit of information that may interest you."

Beckett cleared his throat. The mention of Genevieve in this conversation was not what he had thought their discourse would lead to, and yet, the unsettling pang that twisted his innards left him on edge.

Was Genevieve in some kind of danger? Was she in trouble? What had the nuisance chit been up to that her family did not know about?

"Go on," he said.

"I was standing at the side of the ballroom, talking with several friends regarding very little important information, when I heard Lady Charlotte and Lady Matilda speaking of their disappointment that Lady Genevieve could not attend and had not arrived as agreed.

And yet, when I searched for Lady Genevieve's family, they were not in attendance, which I thought odd. Until..." Wolfson paused. "Lady Matilda mentioned another ball happening tomorrow evening that Lady Genevieve was determined to sneak out to and meet them as agreed."

The foolish minx.

Was that what he caught Genevieve about in the garden earlier? It would certainly explain her interest in roses at midnight. To attend Lady Russel's ball was foolish. But why the desire to attend in the first place? The ball would put her reputation at risk should any of the haute *ton* find out. Was Mr. Venzellon's attendance the reason?

"Is there anything else I should know?" Beckett asked, wondering if he really wanted the answer.

"Well, yes. Later that evening, I heard Mr. Venzellon say he was disappointed the pretty heiress Lady Genevieve was not in attendance. That he had looked forward to continuing his courtship with her." Wolfson tipped his head in the direction of the Americans.

The hairs on the back of Beckett's neck rose. "What else did the blaggard state?" he asked, taking a calming breath.

"You promised to remain calm. Not cause a scene, Tyndall," Wolfson reminded him.

Beckett rubbed a hand over his jaw, nodding. "Of course, I will not. As your friend and a gentleman, I will not outwardly react. Now tell me."

Wolfson sighed. "Apparently, Mr. Venzellons sees Lady Genevieve as his English rose and bride whom he will return to New York with to sit on his trophy shelf. He stated that he looked forward to riding the pretty maiden and breaking her in, only to then, after declaring such a purpose, disappear from the ball with the dowager Russel and not return until an hour or so later, much more disheveled than when he left."

Beckett fisted his hands and set down his crystal glass before he broke it. That would explain where Genevieve was sneaking off to, and he had stopped her foolishness. Did she even like the stiff-rumped fop? Beckett glanced at the American, studying him a moment, and could not see the allure—other than his wealth, supposedly...

"You are upset. I can see the muscle in your temple flexing," Wolfson stated, a concerned frown between his brows.

Wolfson ought to be concerned. For that

matter, Mr. Venzellons ought to be, too. Genevieve could not marry an American. She loved her family too much to move to the other side of the world. He would never see her again, spar with her as they did. Not that he was looking to marry anyone and, least of all, Genevieve, but out of principle, he did not want her to be broken in and ridden by some ass who did not know how to speak about her respectfully.

"Keep this information between us, Wolfson. I shall speak to Lady Genevieve about it, and if I have no success in making her see her interest in Mr. Venzellons is foolhardy, I shall communicate my displeasure to her family. They ought to know how Genevieve, a duke's daughter no less, is being spoken of in town. I doubt they are contemplating a match with Mr. Venzellons, not when so many good English gentlemen would suit much better."

"I wholeheartedly agree. That is why I thought you ought to know. You're the closest person I know of their acquaintance who is not family."

"Thank you, yes, I appreciate the heads-up. Now, shall we go downstairs for a game of billiards?" If he could not hit Mr. Venzellons with a stick, the second-best thing would be a ball.

"Yes, let us go. Best of three games?" Wolfson asked.

"Perfect," Beckett said, standing and walking from the room, but not before glaring at Venzellons for good measure. Whether the pompous ass noticed or not, he did not know, but at least it made him feel better for a moment.

CHAPTER
THREE

Genevieve ran up to Matilda and Charlotte the moment she spied them waiting outside Lord and Lady Whitford's Mayfair home. Large candelabras sat outside the front steps, lighting the way for those invited inside their magnificent home. Carriages bustled along the street, delivering the *ton* to the many entertainments on offer this warm London evening, but only this event interested Genevieve.

Not because she was particularly fond of Lord and Lady Whitford—in fact, she hardly knew the earl and his countess—but the invitation had been directed at her, not her parents, and gave her the perfect opportunity to attend without her mother watching her every move. If she were to catch the interest of Mr. Venzellons, she needed to appear not as the debutante her mama continued to treat her as, but as a woman of one and twenty.

"Oh, I'm so very excited for this evening," Matilda gushed, her cheeks rosy, her long strawberry-blonde hair curling about her shoulders and accentuating her perfect complexion. Charlotte all but bounced beside Matilda, her smile wide and captivating any gentleman who passed them by. Their "good evenings" were deep with meaning and interest.

"We shall have the best of time and without our mamas breathing down our throats," Genevieve said. "We shall only have to contend with them if they find out we attended at all, but alas, the chastisement will be worth it. Certainly, if I'm successful in gaining Mr. Venzellons' interest. Oh, how I would love to live in New York. I heard his home is quite grand, and he has over fifty staff in his city estate alone."

"Not to mention he's handsome and wealthy, enough to satisfy your papa," Charlotte declared.

All true. Mr. Venzellons was suitable and would be her ticket out of England and away from Lord Tyndall and his ilk. Even now, her cheeks warmed at the memory of throwing herself at him like some lost, poor, desperate soul.

With a sigh, she pushed the horrible memory aside and reminded herself that he would've forgotten all about that incident and would not even know what she was talking about should she mention it again. Which, of course, she would not.

But it was time she found a husband. A fourth Season would be dreadful and humiliating for a duke's daughter, and over the past year, her father had lost patience with her, and she did not want to disappoint him anymore. No, it was time to make the best of her situation, do right by her family and marry.

They linked arms and entered the townhouse. The home was by no means as grand as her own or her friends'. They were three heiresses in London, termed The Graces after the goddess sisters of beauty, grace, and charm. However, this evening, they could add another element to their moniker: schemers.

"Oh look, Lord Anson is here this evening, and Lord Wolfson, Matilda," Genevieve mentioned, knowing Matilda harbored feelings toward Lord Wolfson for the past year. Not that the marquess seemed at all aware of the fact. The man was supposedly very much bookish and kept to himself, except when he needed to attend events such as these to keep the mamas of the *ton* happy, his own included.

Genevieve schooled her features when she noticed Mr. Venzellons watching her, a small, teasing smile playing about his handsome mouth. She ignored the urge to check her attire and, instead, excused herself from her friends and stepped in the direction of whom she hoped would be her future husband. Everything was going splendidly before a wall of muscle, and a familiar, sandalwood-smelling gentleman stepped before her and halted her path.

"You're not supposed to be here, Lady Genevieve," the deep baritone growled in her ear. He stepped to the side, his hand secure on her elbow as he walked her to the edge of the room and away from the throng of guests.

Genevieve wrenched free of his hold and stopped herself from stomping on his boot. She glared at him, noting how tall he had become over the past several years. How devastatingly handsome he was in his superfine coat and perfectly tied cravat. Her attention moved over his body, taking in his strong, muscular legs, thanks to the many hours of riding, possibly not always on horses...

Rogue.

She swallowed the jealousy that ripped

through her at the thought of him with anyone else and narrowed her eyes. "You're not my family and cannot tell me what I can and cannot do. I'm at a ball. There is nothing wrong with that." She went to move away, and he ripped her back against him. Her chest grazed his waistcoat, and for a moment, she was left breathless and at sea.

"Everything is wrong with it when your family is not chaperoning you. I shall escort you home this instant."

"You will do no such thing." Genevieve poked Lord Tyndall in the ribs, making him flinch. "Are you truly going to run back to my brother like a good little boy and tell on me? Tell my father what a bad girl I've been?"

Something in Lord Tyndall's eyes darkened, and his mouth pursed into a displeased line. "Do not tempt me, Genevieve."

"I do not believe I have given you leave to use the familiar name my family gifted me, my lord. Unless you would like me to call you Beckett?"

Again, an emotion she could not understand flashed in his gaze before he looked over the ballroom floor with displeasure. "I know why you're here, and I'll not have it. You cannot abandon your family, you must find a husband of good English blood and roots, not sail away to New York and never return."

"What if I want to sail away to New York and never return? What is that to you? Nothing, that is what." Genevieve took a deep breath and reached up to adjust her wig, which was exceedingly itchy this evening. "I do not have to marry anyone from England, and in fact, Mr. Venzellons seems the perfect gentleman with whom I can see myself very happy."

"So you would be happy getting the pox? Because that is what will happen if you marry that rutting animal and return abroad."

She gasped. Surely, that was not true. That would foil all her plans, indeed, and not be what she would wish for, not for anyone. "You lie. Mr. Venzellons does not suffer such an affliction."

"No, perhaps not yet, but he is quite the energetic gentleman about town, if you understand my meaning."

"I understand your meaning perfectly well."

"Do you?" Lord Tyndall crossed his arms and stared at her with amusement, as if he believed she did not. A little wickedness came over her at his highhandedness, his arrogance of her feeble female mind.

She stepped against him, close enough to smell the brandy on his breath. "I know all about what happens between a man and a woman. And his ventures before marriage, I'm certain, will only make the marriage bed more pleasing for me. I know all about the ecstasy that can be reached for both men and women, and in fact, I look forward to feeling what is described as exquisite, otherworldly tremors throughout one's body."

"Dear God." Lord Tyndall paled, his attention dipping to her lips.

Genevieve dampened hers, the overwhelming thought of his mouth on her overriding her good sense and annoyance.

"Who spoke to you of such things? That is not an appropriate conversation for a woman who is still a maid."

Genevieve shrugged, not caring what Lord Tyndall thought. "You should keep your nose out of my business, my lord. I did not ask for you to gate-keep me at any balls and parties, and while you may be a friend of the family, my brother's best friend, we are not. I can do as I wish, and I wish to do Mr. Venzellons." Genevieve frowned at her words, certain they had not come out as she had hoped.

Lord Tyndall cleared his throat. "I would be failing in my duty if I did not take you home."

"Oh no." She wagged her finger at him. "You thwarted my evening the other night bringing home my brother. You shall not do it again. I'm one and twenty, I can do as I please, and I do not need a man telling me otherwise."

"What you need is a good spanking."

Genevieve stared at Lord Tyndall, who stared back, his eyes wide as if he had only just now realized what he had said. An odd fluttering took flight in her stomach, and she raised her chin, refusing to acknowledge what that feeling was.

Nerves. Right?

She would not allow him to make her tense ever again. She had conquered that reaction when around him years ago.

"Good evening, Lord Tyndall. Do keep out of my way, and we shall remain cordial, but if you do not heed my wishes, then we will be enemies, and as one of The Graces, you know what that will mean?"

"What?" He crossed his arms, not giving any of his emotions away bar annoyance.

"As a demigod, I would be forced to kill you." Genevieve smiled sweetly. "Good evening, and goodnight...my lord."

CHAPTER
FOUR

Beckett could easily murder Genevieve right at this moment. He shook his head as she sauntered away without a by your leave, without a care in the world that she had ignored his advice. Not that he would ever hurt her, but if she continued to sneak out of her home in the middle of the night and attend balls and parties her parents were unaware of, she could end up in more trouble than she knew existed.

She was innocent. Even though her conversation this evening and her knowledge of carnal delights was enlightening, more so than he needed to know, it didn't change the fact that what she was doing was wrong and could put her reputation at risk.

He cringed, remembering he'd threatened to spank her ass. He caught sight of her with her friends, her voluptuous gown not giving a hint as to what her ass or legs looked like beneath all that material. Although as shameful as it was, considering she was his best friend's sister, he'd often admired her bodice and the breasts that had formed with adulthood.

He ground his teeth. He should not be imagining anything about her person and how it would appear under her gown. She was off limits. Martin would never forgive him if he dallied with Genevieve. As much as he'd come to fantasize about doing just that...

She had sparked an interest in him for the past two years that he had successfully ignored up until now. But of late, she drew his attention like a moth to a flame each time he was in her company. A maddening, intoxicating affliction he could not cure.

"What is my sister doing here?" Beckett started at the familiar voice before he turned to face Martin. Genevieve's brother glared in the direction of his sister. "Mother forbade her from attending. I was at the breakfast table two days past when that conversation occurred."

"Oh, I do not know what Lady Genevieve is doing here." He feigned ignorance. "Mayhap, you ought to ask her," Beckett offered, glad he had not, in the end, had to disclose Genevieve's whereabouts and nighttime pursuits to her family. A position that put him in a circumstance where he did not think she would ever forgive him. No one liked a snitch.

"Come, we shall ask her together." Before Beckett could stop Martin, Genevieve's brother strode after her, joining her friendship party of three. The ladies' eyes went wide with alarm, their cheeks pale.

"Brother, what are you doing here? I thought you were attending the Thompson's ball," Genevieve stated, her tone light and without concern. Yet the fear that echoed on her pretty features was apparent. Her sibling had caught her, and no nonchalance would clear her way out of this mess.

"I decided to drop in since I knew Tyndall would be here," Martin stated, meeting Beckett's eyes a moment. "But how odd to find you here, sister...unchaperoned." He paused, tapping his chin in thought. "Correct me if I'm wrong, but did not Mama forbid you from attending? Or did my ears deceive me two days past?"

Genevieve sighed, and Beckett felt a pang of pity for her. That women could not attend parties such as the one they now attended would be frustrating if he were in her position. Beckett had little doubt that should he be cushioned from the world as she was, it would drive him mad, if not a little rebellious. He could understand why the Three Graces, as they were known, were breaking the rules.

"You cannot tell me that Lady Matilda and Lady Charlotte should be here either. Do your parents know you're at Lord and Lady Whitford's ball alone and unchaperoned?"

"Well, as to that," Lady Charlotte murmured before Genevieve placed her hand on her friend's arm, stalling her words.

"Do not interrogate my friends, Martin. You have no right. And you arrived by chance." She turned her attention to Tyndall and glared. "I have little doubt how you found out that I'm here. Lord Tyndall proves yet again what a rat he is."

Rat? Had she indeed insulted him just now? "I never told your brother a word of you being here. I had not yet had the time to do so, Lady Genevieve."

She rolled her eyes and crossed her arms. The action lifted her breasts, and Beckett glanced down at the parquetry floor—anywhere but the location that had haunted far too many of his dreams lately. Not to mention, the little mole that sat just above the bodice of her left breast was particularly pretty and shaped like a heart.

"Lord Tyndall has nothing to do with me finding you at a ball you're prohibited from attending. I shall return all three of you to your homes. Please make your excuses to Lady Whitford, and we shall meet in the foyer." Beckett did not say a word. His friend's orders brooked no argument, and it was not his place to say anything to Genevieve, even if he had cautioned her earlier about being here alone.

The sight of tears pooling in Genevieve's eyes, however, was not what he enjoyed seeing, and without thought, he stepped toward her, only for Martin to step between them, ceasing whatever madness had come over him for a moment. What had he been about to do? Pull her into his arms and comfort her? Lead her away and give her kind words of support?

What the hell was wrong with him?

The Three Graces moved toward Lady Whitford, doing as they were bid, and Beckett followed Martin. "I shall escort the ladies home with you, Martin. The ball is less than satisfactory, and I have an early morning meeting with my steward."

"Very good. Let us go," Martin said.

Minutes later, the carriage rolled through Mayfair and deposited Lady Matilda and Lady Charlotte at their respective homes. But when Martin called out the address for Whites,

Beckett frowned. "We're making a detour before heading to Grosvenor Square?" he asked.

"Oh yes, I'm getting off at Whites. Be a good friend and deliver my sister home, Tyndall? You're like a brother to Genevieve, in any case."

Beckett swallowed, knowing only too well that he was, in fact, definitely *not* like a brother to Genevieve, and never had been. When he had first met her, she had been an annoying busybody who followed him and Martin around Curzon's country estate all day, spying on them, wanting to be part of their gang. He had thwarted her every request, and for one reason.

The chit had always looked at him as if she were in love with him and wanted him to kiss her until, one day, she launched herself at his head while alone in the gardens. His first reaction had been to hold out his arm and stop her. That his hand had connected with her forehead and she had been held in that absurd position was an embarrassment he had never recovered from. He couldn't imagine how Genevieve thought of it.

But something told him she had never forgiven him. He had mortified and hurt her feelings. But they had both been children. Could she still blame him for rejecting her kiss?

His gaze dipped to her lips, parted in shock, as the carriage rocked to a halt before the front bow window of Whites. Martin jumped down, calling out the direction for the driver before waving them off without a backward glance.

Damn it all to hell. Beckett would murder Martin, too, if he could get his hands on him.

"I cannot believe you sent for my brother to catch me out this evening. What kind of snitch are you, Tyndall? I've never known an earl to be so ungentlemanly."

Their gazes clashed, and he fought to ignore that when, in a temper, Genevieve's skin was radiant in the moonlight, her eyes bright and burning with vexation. Damn, she had grown into a beautiful, luscious, intelligent, determined woman. She looked like a queen sitting before him in the carriage. Her voluptuous, exquisite gown and white wig, sitting high on her head, gave her an air of stateliness.

"I never sent a missive to your brother. You can believe that or not, but it is the truth."

She scoffed. "And you expect me to accept that?"

"Believe what you want. It is the truth."

The drive to Grosvenor Square was short, and the carriage rolled to a stop before the large Curzon estate, a sprawling Georgian mansion, not a town house that many other residences of the *ton* possessed. While wealthy himself, Duke Curzon exceeded most of the upper ten thousand by hundreds of thousands of pounds, making Genevieve an heiress and catch for anyone brave enough to take the hellcat on.

She wrenched her shawl about her, but instead of leaving the carriage, she leaned toward him, pushing him back into the squabs. "I will not have you thwart my plans this Season, Lord Tyndall, so it would be best if you stayed out of my way."

As much as he tried to, and he desperately did attempt self-control, his gaze dipped to her lips, soft and all but begging for a kiss. Had she ever kissed a man before? A fire, hot and desperate, ignited inside him, and without thought, he slipped a stay curl of her hair behind her ear. "And if I cannot stay out of your way?"

Her attention dipped to his lips, and something in her eyes darkened. "Then I shall make you," she said, pushing the carriage door open and jumping down, before disappearing through the front gate of her house and out of sight.

But never, damn it all to hell, out of his mind.

CHAPTER
FIVE

Genevieve slumped against the front door, heart racing a million beats a breath. She played over and over again what had just occurred in the carriage. She had argued with Lord Tyndall, nothing uncommon about that, but what had happened just before she jumped out? Or a better question was, what on earth had *almost* happened between them.

She bit her lip and pushed away from the door, heading for her room.

The house was quiet, save for the footman, who sat near the entrance and did not question where she had been or with whom. He would not dare, but still, she attempted to look nonplussed as she started up the stairs, as if coming back from a ball without the chaperonage of her mama was commonplace.

When she entered her room, her maid Louise was waiting for her. Quickly undressing and slipping on a clean shift, she climbed into bed. Sleep would be elusive until she sorted out what had transpired between her and Tyndall in her mind.

Beckett...

Never in her life, not even when she had made a fool of herself in front of Lord Tyndall all those years ago, had her body craved a kiss as much as it did but moments ago. Something in Tyndall's eyes told her his thoughts had strayed to that consideration, too.

A first for her and a situation she was entirely at sea how to proceed with.

Her maid bustled about the room as Genevieve's mind fussed about Tyndall—what to do about that man? He was her brother's best friend and family friend, too. Her parents were very fond of the earl. He was a charming flirt to everyone except her. Many ladies adored Tyndall, seeking him out at balls and parties. He certainly never was at a loss for dance partners.

But then, she had never been on the receiving end of what she could only term as... *desire.*

Had he wanted her in that carriage? Her body said yes, but her mind could not comprehend such an outcome. If he did desire her in a romantic sense, maybe she could use that power to her advantage and drag Tyndall about society like an obedient puppy. Do as she planned and keep her family out of her way while she tried to secure Mr. Venzellons.

Genevieve shook her head at the fanciful thought. It would never come to fruition. Tyndall would have no part in her seeking a husband.

No, she would have to avoid him somehow, find out what entertainment he was to attend, and ensure she was not. How else was she to enjoy the Season with her friends without his interruptions?

Tomorrow evening was the Fraser masque ball, and she was determined to attend with her best friends so she would not have to endure Tyndall's aggravating reminders of what she wasn't allowed to do.

The night was all planned. Each of her friends had been given approval to stay at each other's homes, yet none of them were staying where they said.

Charlotte had stolen the key from her brother's room to the small lodging house he rented when he wished for privacy. Since he was away in Scotland attending their highland estate, he wasn't in town to do anything about their plan.

Their one night in London would be the best of times and perhaps their only chance to gain a little freedom in the otherwise strict lifestyle that they endured, especially now that Tyndall was aware of her ventures.

Tyndall attended three balls this evening and still had not seen the The Graces anywhere. He did another loop of the Southcott ballroom and decided they were not in attendance.

The sight of Viscount Anson caught his attention, and he joined him, glad he was alone. "Good evening, Anson. Are you enjoying the ball?" he asked, knowing Anson had an infatuation with Lady Charlotte that he refused to act on being that he was shy and she was not.

"Tyndall, good evening to you. I have been enjoying the ball, but am about to head off. Another function to attend."

"Really? I've been to three already. Surely, there cannot be more on this evening."

"Oh, but there is. The Fraser masque ball. Did you not receive an invite?"

No, he had not, and he knew the reason

why. It was being hosted by Dowager Lady Fraser, a woman he had refused a liaison with since her husband, much older than himself, was his friend. He may be a rogue, but still, he had some morals.

Was that where Genevieve was this evening? Surely, after his warning last night, she would not be so brazen as to attend a masque without the chaperonage of her family.

The chit was a danger to herself.

"I did not." Beckett frowned, wondering how he could attend.

"I have an invitation, and it allows me to bring a friend if you want to accompany me. I'm leaving now if you're happy to go."

Beckett slapped Anson on the shoulder and gestured for him to lead the way. "Let us go. A masque sounds an enjoyable way to end the night."

It didn't take long for the carriage to drop them off before the Fraser Georgian town house just shy of Mayfair. Upon entering, they saw the rooms were full of guests. Their masks, wigs, and gowns enabled many to attend without anyone knowing whom they were speaking to. Anson had procured a masque, but Beckett, having no invite, had not. Not that it mattered too much. A few did not wear much at all, nevertheless a masque.

"I'm going to do a turn about the rooms."

"Right, you are." Anson headed off in the opposite direction to him.

Beckett took in the room, but after moving through the many spaces open for the ball, ease came over him. Confident Lady Genevieve wasn't in attendance here either.

Mayhap, the troubling chit, had taken heed of his threat and remained home. That was always a possibility.

The house was dark. Only a few candles burned in each room, giving the ball an air of mystery and seduction. Beckett stood beside the ballroom floor and sighed, exacerbated but hopeful that Genevieve wasn't here. The masque did look amusing, and he would hate to have to babysit his friend's little sister or escort her back to Mayfair and miss the party. The last thing he wished to do was be alone with her in a carriage again.

Beckett strolled the room's edges, smiling at several women who noted his attendance, not that he knew who they were, their masks kept their identity a secret.

His steps faltered. His mouth dried at seeing a woman he had never noticed before. She wore a masque over her eyes that covered her nose. Her black hair was straight and slipped over her shoulders and sat upon two perfect breasts that made his mouth water. He moved toward her, glad she was alone. He clasped her gloveless hand, bowing and kissing her in welcome.

"Good evening, my lady. You must tell me who you are this night. Your costume has me enthralled." His body prickled with awareness.

She grinned at him, her eyes flashing with surprise at his words. Was the lady unused to such compliments? He rarely saw women in society with hair such as this woman's, but her height and teasing lips painted rouge, made his blood simmer.

"Good evening, my lord. I'm a secret if you must know. And you?" she asked, her eyes moving over his body like a caress. He bit his tongue, feeling her inspection as if she had slipped her hands under his shirt and stroked his flesh.

He shivered at the thought. "I'm Lord Tyndall, my lady, but you are beauty personified. I must know your name."

She threw him a teasing grin and waved a finger before his nose before that same finger slipped over his lips, tracing them. "No names this evening, even though I know who you are, Lord Tyndall." Her voice was low and seductive. There was something familiar in the tenor, yet he could not place it.

Mayhap he had met her before. There was a chance they had even been intimate in the past. He'd certainly had many lovers.

"Dance with me?" he asked, lifting her hand and kissing her fingers a second time.

"If you insist, my lord. It would be my pleasure."

And his also.

CHAPTER
SIX

Genevieve fought not to quiver at Lord Tyndall's touch as he led her onto the dance floor. The sound of a waltz drifted from the minstrel's galley as Tyndall pulled her into his arms. The sensation of being wrapped in protective, strong arms ran through her. She took a calming breath and fought to appear to be the sophisticated stranger who had caught his eye rather than the scared, innocent debutante she was.

The scent of sandalwood, mixed with lavender, teased her senses and did little to help her nerves. Damn, the man smelled good enough to devour.

What was she doing touching Tyndall so intimately? Running her finger across his lips indeed. Had she lost all sense of decorum and, well, sense?

If he ever found out that she, Lady Genevieve, was the mystery woman behind the masque, he may well indeed feel inclined to take her over his lap and spank her. Not to mention, he would undoubtedly tell her parents of her escapades without them.

"I must know who you are. It is unfair that you know my name, but I've yet to learn yours." His mischievous grin made her stomach flutter, and she bit her lip, unsure how to proceed. She was never one to flirt and had not learned the art, but somehow, this situation called for it.

Oh dear, how to not fail miserably and embarrass herself more.

His eyes swirled with a determination she wasn't sure she could hold off. His attention settled on her mouth, and she swallowed, nerves overcoming her composure.

"I don't believe that is the point of a masque ball, my lord. In fact, you should have one on yourself to remain anonymous."

"I came from the Southcott ball and did not have time to change."

The very ball she had been invited to, but her mama, in her snobbery, had deemed Lord and Lady Southcott not high enough in society to host the Duke and Duchess Curzon. So she, too, had to decline the invitation. Not that it mattered now. Now when she was at Lady Fraser's masque ball instead and dancing with Tyndall.

She ought to loathe him forever. He embarrassed her beyond redemption in her youth, but still, she was not blind, nor could she ignore that his lordship was one of the most handsome gentlemen in London.

His teeth were ideal, his nose straight but not imposing, and his brows arched perfectly above his large almond-shaped eyes. Not to mention, his hair was thick, with a sweet waviness to it. He would make any woman's head turn.

The problem, of course, was that Tyndall knew his effect on women and loved every moment of being worshipped by the fairer sex.

"Well, it is unfortunate you cannot partake in the mystery of the night, but that does not mean that I will not continue to do so." She spoke with a lowered voice, one she had practiced and intended to use when around Mr. Venzellons, who unfortunately was not present this evening.

But that did not matter. She would surely see him at the Miller's outdoor ball tomorrow evening and could practice her more mature, seductive voice on him then.

Lord Tyndall spun her about during the

dance, and Genevieve laughed, enjoying this amusing and teasing side of her enemy she had never seen before. He would not be so if he knew who was in his arms. Oh, how angry he would be. Probably drag her from the ball without a backward glance and little care as to who saw.

The thought of him not knowing who she was sparked a mischievous idea in her mind, and the more she dwelled on it, the more she wished to see just how far she could push his interest. She had yet to enjoy her first kiss, and who better to kiss than an old family friend who would never hurt her or ask for more than she was willing to give?

"You are one mystery I would like to solve."

Genevieve's body shivered at his words. The deep timbre that brooked no argument was as intoxicating as his pretty visage. Was he trying to seduce her really? He did not know who she was at all. Was this how those termed rakes and rogues were around women they desired? The idea that she was receiving such interest was dizzying and all too alluring to stop now.

"Well, you cannot unveil me, but perhaps I can gift you one boon." Had she really said those words? Could she follow through on her idea and offer Tyndall a kiss? Her first?

"If that one boon is all I'm to receive this night, please let it be that I get to kiss your sweet lips. You're so beautiful. I must taste you just once."

Genevieve swallowed and rallied her nerves. She had never kissed a man in her life, and now she needed to appear as if she knew what she was about.

Maybe he thought she was a woman who sold her trade on Drury Lane. Or a widow of a wealthy, titled gentleman. She was neither of those things, of course. She was a maid, an inexperienced woman in her third Season who had yet to have her first kiss.

She didn't want to appear as if she were untutored and green. Dear Lord, that would be another embarrassment at the hands of Tyndall she would never recover from. And yet, she had offered and needed to be assertive. How hard could it be to kiss a man? All would be well if she merely copied what he did and did not panic.

The dance came to an end, and conveniently, Lord Tyndall swirled them to a stop away from the ballroom floor in a quiet corner no one else occupied.

"So you wish to kiss me, Lord Tyndall. How thrilling," she teased, stepping close, another action she presumed all ladies did before kissing a man. His eyes darkened, and his arms snaked about her waist, wrenching her close.

She gasped, not expecting him to do such a thing or the reaction her body had to his touch. Heat and need settled in parts of her she did not know existed, and hunger took hold of her person.

Her hands fluttered to his chest, the hardened muscles, his beating heart warming the palms of her hands. Without fear, she slipped her arms over his shoulders and played with the hair at his nape.

"Now is your chance if you wish to do so," she stated, hoping he would not relent and flee, disappointing her.

Without a word of warning, his mouth crashed against hers. His lips were soft but demanded a response. Genevieve gasped. The feel of his lips on hers startled her, enthralled too. He moved against her, seducing her with his wicked kiss. His tongue teased, a sensation so different and sweet that she copied his lead.

She pressed against him, her body acting without thought. He walked them backward until her back hit the wall. Finally, she could feel all of him, his hardened muscles, his lust for her that pressed into her stomach.

His hands cupped her bottom, pulling her against his body. His manhood felt immense, and Genevieve fumbled to remain standing. Was she doing this to him? Making him lose his self-control?

Any moment now, he would wrench away with the realization of whom he was kissing. Demand to know if she knew what she was doing. Force her to tell her parents about her outrageous behavior.

But after several more devastating kisses, he did not.

Instead, he groaned, the sound laced with need and longing. Begged for her name and made her almost whisper it back.

She could not tell him who she was. This night, this kiss would forever be her secret, and his to always wonder about.

A warm sensation built between her legs, and she pressed against his manhood. He undulated against her, making her feel wonderful, pushing her toward a sensation that promised to be worth the risk.

He sucked in a breath, his kiss deepened, became frantic and savage. At some point, her fingers slipped into his hair, fisting his locks, holding him close as if to never let him go.

And right then, Genevieve certainly wished she never had to.

"Genevieve, where are you?" she distantly

heard Matilda call before her friend's shocked squeak sounded nearby.

Lord Tyndall wrenched her away and she stumbled before righting her footing. He stared at her, his eyes wide, his cheeks pink, his lips swollen from their kiss. His attention moved from her to Matilda, who no longer wore a masque.

"I'm sorry, Genevieve. I did not know you were... You were..."

She stared at Lord Tyndall and raised her chin, relishing yet regretting the horror written on her enemy's visage.

"Lady Genevieve?" he rasped, his voice bewildered.

With no other option and knowing she could not lie, she grinned. "The one and only, Lord Tyndall." She stepped close to him and ignored his slight flinch. "I suppose the kiss I longed for at fifteen was finally granted. Maybe I should thank you." Genevieve managed the words with a casual air, but she did not feel so nonchalant. "It was better than I thought it would be," she declared before linking arms with Matilda and leaving Lord Tyndall gaping after them in their wake.

CHAPTER
SEVEN

What the hell had he just done! Beckett touched his lips, his body vibrating from the kiss he had just shared.

But Lady Genevieve?

No, it could not have been her. He could not have been kissing that termagant—his best friend's sister.

Dear God, Martin would have his head on a pike if he learned what had occurred this evening.

He took a calming breath and watched as Lady Genevieve and Matilda left the ball, Genevieve's hips swaying suggestively as she made her way through the throng of guests. He had never presumed that it was Genevieve in his arms. The scent of jasmine that seduced his senses should have been his first hint, but so lost in her charms, he had not put two and two together.

He'd never held Genevieve before tonight and had not the slightest inkling that the seductive minx in his arms was anyone but a stranger.

It could not have been Genevieve.

Oh dear Lord, what was he going to do? And more importantly, how the hell was he going to tell Martin of his actions tonight? To do so could spell the end of their friendship, which he was loath to lose. Martin had always been there for him after his parents had died in a carriage during his childhood. The Duke and Duchess Curzon had opened their home to him each Christmas and school holidays. When he was not at Eton or later Cambridge, there wasn't a time when he wasn't part of the Curzon family dynamic.

They would be disappointed if they found out he had returned their kindness by molesting their innocent daughter.

A woman who was still a debutante in truth. A woman who was a maid, unattached, and unmarried. The image of him holding her against the wall, feeling her body press against his. The masque ball had allowed the guests to wear gowns of their choosing, and this evening, Genevieve had worn a far too revealing one.

Gone were the large, billowing skirts, tight bodices, and small sleeves, and in their place stood a gown that involved very little material or imagination as to what lay beneath.

He ran a hand through his hair, at a loss how to fix his faux pas. She had been a goddess, and one he had been unable to resist.

He swallowed the bile in his throat. Had anyone seen him act without decorum? Did they know who she was the entire time he'd kissed her?

Beckett looked around, and although no one was watching him, he could not help but feel they all knew what he had done.

Wanting away out, he strode from the room, luckily catching a hackney cab as he stepped out of the town house. However, he would not go home. He needed to speak to Genevieve if he could catch her in time.

The carriage started through Mayfair, and the sight of Lady Genevieve and her friends stumbling out of the carriage laughing and heading toward Lady Charlotte's brother's lodging rooms had him call his vehicle to a stop.

He watched them, dumbfounded, as they

entered the building, certainly not heading toward their respective homes.

What the hell were these women up to with their unruly behavior?

He jumped down, threw the driver a coin, and went after the three of them, catching them at the lodging door.

"What the hell are you three about? Are you trying to ruin yourselves and your families?"

All three let out a little squeal. Lady Charlotte and Matilda rushed into the room, but Genevieve stood her ground and faced him. He expected no less.

"Lord Tyndall, a pleasure as always." She attempted to enter the rooms, but he closed the door, halting her departure.

"Lady Genevieve, a word, if you please."

She raised her brow and watched him with a confidence he couldn't believe she possessed after her actions this evening. The woman had no shame.

But then, there was no shame in a stolen kiss or two unless that kiss was with him.

"Lady Genevieve, do you have a response to what occurred at the Fraser masque just now? Are you going to continue to ignore what we just did?" he asked, unable to hide the astonishment in his voice. The woman was maddening and becoming more so with every minute he spent with her.

"Nothing occurred worth noting. We kissed. Refrain from getting yourself so worked up, my lord. I'm not asking you to marry me, now am I?"

He shut his mouth with a snap. Had she dismissed him without a by your leave, without an ounce of regret or shame?

He had never been dismissed and wasn't entirely sure he liked the feeling. He ignored the warning voice in his head that maybe it was because Genevieve had dismissed him so quickly that he disliked it so.

"You cannot be going out as you are and kissing random gentlemen at masque balls. What if I had pushed for more?"

"I knew who you were and, therefore, knew you would not force more upon me. Not if I didn't wish it." She patted his arm condescendingly. "You were nothing more than a person I knew and trusted, even if we're not the closest of friends, whom I could practice upon. I'm now aware of the kissing mechanics, and thank you for the tutelage."

"What does that mean?" he asked, pulling her to a stop when she went to enter the lodging.

"It means I can now kiss the man I wish to and know what I'm doing."

"And what man is that?" Beckett's words came out harsher, more desperate than he would like, and he collected himself. "You cannot kiss anyone else. I forbid it. You cannot kiss any man unless that man is your husband."

Genevieve crossed her arms and raised her brows. She looked so lofty and disapproving, but she should not. It was himself who ought to be so. "I intend for the man I kiss to turn into my husband, so there will be little harm to come of it. But do not forbid me again, my lord. You're forgetting your place."

"I'm an earl, a friend of your family. My place is protecting you."

"You're not my keeper. Stay out of my way."

He closed the space between them, determined to chastise her and threaten her with exposure if she did not do as he said. Yet the moment he stepped near, her sweet scent teased his senses. Her face tipped toward his, and her lips parted in expectation.

His mind pivoted to their kiss earlier in the night, catapulting back to how much he had enjoyed it.

Damn her and her pretty face.

"Genevieve," he whispered, unable to think

of anything else to say. In the darkened corridor of the lodging house, she looked like a tempting fallen angel with her dark hair, temptation personified to torture him for eternity.

"You do not wish to do this, Tyndall. You will regret kissing me again if that is what you mean to do."

Her words pulled him out of his strange trance, and as if a bucket of cold water had been tossed over his head, he stepped back, securing her reputation and his senses. "I fear you have left me with no choice. I will have to inform your father of your nightly pursuits."

She chuckled, not the expected response, and he ground his teeth. The woman was beyond help.

"If you should utter one word, I shall tell Papa that you kissed me, clutched at my bottom, and left me in fear of my reputation. I will demand that you marry me to save my blushes in society. So if you do not wish to find yourself at the altar, Lord Tyndall, be a good boy and keep our secret. Because you know what I say is true. The secret is not just mine to keep. Not now that you've included yourself in my evening." She paused, grinning. "I do not think you wish to marry me unless you're harboring some deep, hidden feelings you're ignoring."

Was the chit taunting him? Damn her to Hades, had she always been such a nightmare?

Yet she was right. He could not say a word unless he was wholly truthful and offered for her hand. Their kiss had been a fiery passion that had swept his feet from under him. Why had he clutched at her? Why had he been drawn to her in the first place and kissed her as he had?

"Very well, I shall keep our secret, but who is the man you wish to marry? I should hope it is not Mr. Venzellons. He's far from suitable, as I have pointed out before."

"Ah, well, that is my decision and concern. And do not fret, for Papa will ensure I make a good match, and that is all I'll say on the matter." Genevieve reached for the doorknob to leave him.

Beckett watched, ensured she entered safely inside the lodgings and left. He swore and mumbled to himself the many ways he would strangle Genevieve and stop her scandalous endeavors. Yet he did not know how to do the latter. She had always been headstrong and resolved, but he'd never known how much.

Not until tonight. Now, he was only too aware.

CHAPTER
EIGHT

Genevieve sat in the small drawing room of the lodging house. Matilda and Charlotte waited silently while Genevieve's ladies' maid finished placing the tray of hot tea and biscuits before them.

The moment they were alone, Matilda rounded on her. "You shared a kiss with Lord Tyndall last evening. What happened for that to transpire, Genevieve! We must know! We're dying of the frustration of not living vicariously through you."

Genevieve poured the tea and placed a lump of sugar in each cup before answering. Her mind still did not know how to comprehend what had occurred herself, nevertheless explain it to her friends.

"I do not know what happened. I was at the ball as you were, and then Lord Tyndall was before me, demanding to know who I was. He seemed odd and not like the frosty earl he normally is around me. I wanted to taunt him a little. You know...see how much I could tease him and, well..."

"Oh yes, well indeed. We know only too well how much you both love bickering. But you kissed Tyndall at a ball. Do you think anyone knew who you were?" Charlotte asked, a concerned frown between her brows.

Genevieve shrugged. "I do not think so. Not even Lord Tyndall knew who I was until Matilda came calling for me and gave me away."

Matilda had the grace to look sheepish. "I do apologize. I came around the corner looking for you and called your name in shock when I saw you in an embrace with Lord Tyndall. An embrace I must say was quite scandalous indeed. He had his hands on your bottom."

A shiver of awareness ran through Genevieve, and she nodded, only too aware of where Tyndall's hands had been and what he had been grinding against her body. Her stomach quivered even now.

Would they ever repeat such an interaction? Disappointment stabbed at her that they would not. A shame, for she dearly enjoyed having a man in her arms and teasing her as he had. Was that the sensation that everyone called desire? Did she now desire Lord Tyndall, or could she experience such a reaction with anyone?

"Yes, he did indeed."

"Were you scandalized or did you relish his pawing?" Charlotte asked, interest shining in her bright-blue eyes.

Genevieve bit back a grin, but even she knew she, too, looked like the cat who found the cream. "I must admit that I've never been held in such a way by a man, and certainly did not expect Tyndall to be the first. But now that he has, the sensations that ran through my body, ladies, well, even now my skin feels all prickly, and my stomach tumbles with nerves. I enjoyed his pawing more than I thought I ever would. He is quite the seducer, but he was also terribly angry with me. You saw his face when he accosted me at the door just before. I fear he will tell my parents."

"He would not dare. Not after he ravished you before everyone?" Matilda said.

"What did he say to you? I hope you told him he has no right to chide you like a child," Charlotte stated.

"We argued. He was mortified it was me he kissed." Annoyance ran through her. Had he not enjoyed the kiss as much as she did?

Blasted rogue did not know when something extraordinary was in his arms. "He threatened to tell my parents, but I reminded him that should he, I would demand Papa make Lord Tyndall marry me out of duty, which cooled his threat to be a snitch. Even so, I think he was more mad at himself than anything else. There were—let me say—signs that his lordship was not immune to my charms."

She chuckled, and so did her friends before she rallied her thoughts. "But I did end up explaining that I'm not looking to his lordship for marriage, that I have my sights on someone completely different, and that he should keep his mouth closed and allow me to continue on with my Season as I have so far."

"And did he agree?" Charlotte asked.

"I'm not sure," she answered truthfully. "I think he will not tell a soul that he kissed me, but he wanted to know who I wanted to pursue. I did not tell him. I need to learn more about Mr. Venzellons before I decide if he would be a suitable husband. And he does live in New York, which would mean leaving England and you both, which, of course, I would miss you both terribly. There is a lot to consider."

"But then, Mr. Venzellons is deadly handsome and rich. Your life in America would not be so very different from yours here, and being the daughter of a duke, you would be quite a popular guest in society. You would suit your new life and do very well abroad."

"Perhaps." Genevieve, as much as she needed a husband now, hadn't thought much about leaving the country of her birth to enjoy a marriage. A pang of sadness settled in her soul at the thought of leaving her beloved England and her two friends. She would be unlikely to return home very much, and would miss Charlotte and Matilda dreadfully, as well as her troublesome brother, just a little bit.

The image of Lord Tyndall flashed before her eyes, and she knew she would miss his lordship, possibly most of all. Not that she ought to miss him. For years, he was a cad and had made it clear that he found her more annoying than alluring.

Except for last evening...

That had indeed put a little wrench in her plans. It made her wonder if Tyndall would see her in a new light after their kiss. He certainly seemed to enjoy her. She bit her lip, wanting to feel the enticement, the passion he evoked.

"You ought to forget about Tyndall and concentrate on Mr. Venzellons. Maybe there will also be an opportunity for you to kiss the gentleman. Decide if you like his kisses better than Tyndall's, and then the choice will be easy. If you enjoyed Tyndall more, knowing he is your enemy and has been for years, then perhaps staying in England and finding a husband here would be best instead of leaving for a new country where you'll be alone with your mistake. But...if Mr. Venzellons sparks a desire in you that will not be sated, you should pursue him. I'm certain your body and soul will tell you which direction you ought to choose," Charlotte said with a decisive nod.

"I think you're right of course. I will not rush into my decision. We have the Millers ball tomorrow evening. I'm certain both gentlemen will be present. It will allow me to see how interested Mr. Venzellons is in my hand. If Lord Tyndall does not cause any more trouble and keeps out of my way, I will be able to make a decision more easily."

"He will not bother you again. As you said, had he known who you were, he would never have kissed you," Matilda said.

A disappointing truthful statement. Lord Tyndall had looked mortified, sickened to his stomach, when he'd realized he had kissed his best friend's sister. His enemy.

She may be a woman, but he would forever see her as a nuisance, a troublesome child who followed him, mooning over his good looks and acceptability. Well, she was done being bottle-headed. She had a new gentleman to court, which would hopefully prove worthwhile. She would know her choice was correct if she felt the familiar desire Tyndall evoked with Venzellons.

Lord Tyndall loathed his mistake in kissing her. Here's hoping Mr. Venzellons would be different.

CHAPTER NINE

With a maid in tow, Genevieve pushed the door of Hatchards open and walked into her favorite bookstore in London. She walked the many rooms, looking for a good gothic romance she may like, and yet her mind would not dispel the image of Lord Tyndall kissing her. Or the mortification on his handsome features when he realized who was in his arms.

Was she so dreadful to kiss?

Surely not.

She stared at a row of books, their titles and genres blurred, as her mind dwelled on what had happened between her and Tyndall. He was her brother's best friend, her enemy, and her childhood bully.

And yet...he was also the first man who had

ever made her feel anything for the opposite sex.

Why could she not have felt nothing with him?

Damn man was a pebble in her shoe.

"Lady Genevieve, how fortunate to meet you here."

She turned and stared at Mr. Venzellons, who smiled at her as if she were some strange creature he had discovered. She dipped into a curtsy out of politeness and returned his smile. "Mr. Venzellons, good afternoon. I did not think to run into you at Hatchards." Her father had introduced her earlier in the Season, but he'd been frustratingly distant since then.

Considering that she considered him the most handsome and suitable gentleman to pursue, she ought to have made more effort to gain conversation.

As it stood, she knew very little about him. His likes and dislikes, what books he enjoyed, anything. She didn't want to admit it, but maybe Lord Tyndall had a point that she ought to get to know Mr. Venzellons better before she desired him as a husband.

"I have just purchased *The History of Tom Jones, a Foundling*." Mr. Venzellons held up the book to prove he indeed purchased the tome. He turned and inspected the shelves she stood before. "Are you searching for the anatomy of foxes? You seem to be before the zoology sciences."

Heat kissed Genevieve's cheeks, and she finally read the spines of the books, confirming that she was indeed in the animal sciences area.

She let out an awkward chuckle. "No, in fact, you find me daydreaming, and I just happened to be daydreaming before this genre."

"Well, if you require some fresh air, may I be so bold as to walk you a little way to your carriage?"

"I do. As a matter of fact, I was heading to Hyde Park afterward for a stroll with my friends, but I could use some company if it interests you."

"Perhaps I could escort you there, and we shall enjoy a walk together if I'm not so bold in asking."

Pleasure thrummed through Genevieve at his kind offer. Did this mean that Mr. Venzellons favored her and had finally commenced his pursuit of her hand? Why else would he seek her out here in the bookshop? He could have merely left after buying his book.

"I would like that very much." He held out his arm, and she linked hers with his, bidding the clerk a good afternoon before leaving the shop. Jeffries, her driver, opened the door to the carriage and set down the steps. "To Hyde Park, Jeffries. Mr. Venzellons is joining me on my walk this afternoon."

"Of course, Lady Genevieve." Jeffries' attention moved to Mr. Venzellons, and if she were not mistaken, her driver didn't hide his critique of her escort.

She gathered her skirts and stepped into the carriage, glad she had asked for the top to be down this afternoon, especially since she was now with Mr. Venzellons. Her maid sat at the back of the carriage, and they were soon rumbling along the cobbled street toward the park.

"I understand you're from New York," she said. "Is it much different there than here? I hear it is a growing and bustling city that will soon rival London."

He leaned back against the leather squabs, his smile a little mocking for her taste. She pushed down the concern that perhaps he wasn't as charming as she thought, and was determined to give him a second chance.

"New York is grand indeed with many opportunities. I have succeeded there beyond my imagination, making a fortune that I'm not afraid to admit may rival your dowry."

Genevieve blinked owlishly, not quite believing he had said those words. But then, Americans did boast, or so she had heard. Perhaps if she were his wife, she would soon become accustomed to such habits.

"And where did you come from before moving to New York and making your way there?"

"Oh, I lived in the Province of North Carolina, a grueling lifestyle to be sure, but I found gold, quite a lot of it, in fact, while prospecting, enabling me to move to the city. I have commenced building a home in Manhattan where I would like to raise a family one day if God wills it. I'm sure there will soon be banking and trade in the city. It is growing at an astronomical rate that anyone would be impressed with."

"Well, it does sound exciting."

Mr. Venzellons smiled. He was handsome, with clean, straight teeth, cutting cheekbones, and the darkest blue eyes she had seen in quite some time. And yet, the butterflies she hoped to feel did not arise. No matter how long she stared at the pretty man.

The thought of kissing him held no appeal. Why though was a mystery. He was interesting, had a unique accent, and wasn't unpleasant to be around, but there was no spark, no fire behind his eyes, and she certainly felt the same as he appeared.

What on earth was wrong with her?

Perhaps those wants and needs would appear in time, the more she came to know him...

The carriage rumbled along Piccadilly before turning onto Park Lane and into the park. They drove in silence for a time before Jeffries pulled the carriage onto the grass and jumped down to help them alight.

Genevieve slipped on a broad-rimmed hat, took Jeffries' hand, and stepped down, taking Mr. Venzellons' arm as they started to walk.

They were near the Serpentine and moved onto a graveled path circling the lake. They would not be doing a complete rotation today, but it would give them time to speak without interruption.

"The park is beautiful, much like my company this afternoon."

Genevieve chuckled, enjoying such off-the-cuff compliments. Although she received many and had been quite popular those last two Seasons, they were from gentlemen she held no interest in. It was pleasant to hear a compliment from a relative stranger. "Thank you, Mr. Venzellons. That is very kind of you."

She reached for her fan that hung off her wrist and opened it, fanning herself.

"Are you warm in that dress? To see the fashions that women must endure makes me sweat. Not that my own suit is not warm, but your skirt must have yards of fabric to its name."

Genevieve looked down at her dress, certain Mr.Venzellons was correct. There were more yards in her skirt than she cared to know. But speaking of one's garments was not the thing to do, and she debated whether she ought to school him on proper etiquette. But then, they were alone, besides her maid, who followed a few steps behind. What did it hurt to speak the truth sometimes?

"It is very warm. Perhaps we can stick to the shade of the trees," she suggested, pointing her fan to a copse of trees lining the lake.

"Of course." Mr. Venzellons escorted her to shadier paths, but the sight of a boat on the lake caught her attention. Her steps stopped, and Mr. Venzellons almost tripped into her at the suddenness of her halting.

"Something the matter, Lady Genevieve?"

"No, nothing at all." She started toward the trees again, and yet, something was certainly very wrong. Why was Lord Tyndall out on the lake in a boat, but not with some nameless woman she did not care about or care to know, but one of her best friends in all the world, Lady Charlotte?

CHAPTER
TEN

Beckett entered Whites later the next afternoon. He stopped halfway up the stairs and took a calming breath, needing to tamper down the ire, vexation, and blasted desire that still ran through him after kissing Genevieve.

Not to mention, seeing her this afternoon had set his hackles to rise.

And he could lay all of his troubles at one man's door.

Her brother's.

His best friend.

Continuing, he spied Martin lounging on a settee, feet on the armrest, and paper over his face. No doubt the blaggard—and he was a blaggard—was sleeping off the night of excessiveness.

He stormed over to Martin and ripped the

paper off his face, but if he expected Martin to startle awake and protest being assaulted, it was not to be. The fiend remained asleep, his light snore gifting those in his presence.

"Martin, wake up," he ordered, kicking the leg of the chair, but to no avail. "Martin, wake up," he said a little louder this time, and still the man slept.

"You won't wake him. He was at Vauxhall earlier tonight and only stumbled in an hour or so ago. Said he was determined to sleep off his indulgences," Lord Smythe called, laughing at Martin's excesses.

Beckett looked around and lost patience. He spied a glass of water and picked it up, splashing it over Martin's face. He slammed the crystal onto a nearby sideboard for good measure, glad to see at last some small motion that he'd woken up his friend.

"What in the blazes..." Martin mumbled, sitting up.

"We need to speak, and you need to get a hold of your senses right this moment, or I'll find another glass of water and throw it at your face a second time."

Martin blinked, confusion muddying his dark-green eyes—eyes very similar to Genevieve's—before he frowned. "What the blazes, Tyndall. I was having a nap. You know never to wake a man when he's napping? And certainly not your best friend. What sort of unkindness is this?" he protested.

Beckett looked at him, nonplussed. "Do you have any idea what I saw this afternoon?"

"What?" Martin said, raising his arm for a footman, who quickly deposited a whisky, Martin's choice of beverage.

"Your sister, walking arm in arm with Mr. Venzellons. The American, if you recall. What brazenness does the man have escorting your sister about London as if he is her equal?"

"He's rich, is he not? That makes him equal enough."

"She's a duke's daughter, and he's the son of nobody knows who."

"He made his fortune, and from what I know of him, seems pleasant enough. If he has his sights set on Genevieve, then all the better. She needs to marry and soon. Do you know she's in her third Season? Mama and Papa are beyond exasperated about what to do, and so am I. She's pretty enough and has a very handsome dowry. You would have thought someone would have snapped her up by now."

"She's not food for the hungry to be devoured," Beckett snarled, slumping back in his chair and glaring at his friend. "Lady Genevieve ought to marry a proper Englishman of good standing and noble blood. Not some American who found gold."

"Oh yes, he mentioned to me this afternoon that he had found quite a substantial amount of it, enough to last him a lifetime."

"And if he's lying, and you give your sister away to him, and she suffers for your bad choice, what then?"

"Then I suppose she would come home... but does it matter?" Martin downed his whisky. "And anyway, what is it to you? She's not your sister."

His friend's question caught him off guard, and for several moments, he did not know how to answer. "I do not trust the man, and I have heard he speaks crassly about Lady Genevieve, wanting her for himself, to bed her. You should not want that for your sister."

"Ahh, but Tyndall, it is not my choice. My father will make that decision, and if he finds no fault with Mr. Venzellons, then nor will I."

"You are my oldest and closest friend. You must speak to Genevieve and caution her to choose carefully and not with haste. Marriage is a lifelong commitment, and I do not believe you would even enjoy seeing her unhappy and disappointed."

"Well, of course not, but if she were walking

with Mr. Venzellons, what am I to do about it? She's of age, old enough to know what is good and bad and right and wrong for herself. If she wishes to accept the man's suit and eventual proposal, I shall not be the one to stop it."

Damned if Beckett would allow such a travesty. But then, what could he do about it?

He had seen the moment Genevieve spied him, and the distaste, annoyance, and loathing that settled on her pretty face let him know that she would not listen to him or take his advice.

But after their kiss, damn it all to hell, a kiss that had haunted him, he had done something so out of character that even now, he could not believe it.

He had asked Lady Charlotte, who had been walking near the Serpentine, for an outing in a boat. Only to gain more information on Lady Genevieve and her suitor. A mistake, for Charlotte, loyal to Genevieve, had not said a word and was vague and unhelpful in every way.

"I hope this overreaction to my sister and Mr. Venzellons does not indicate your feelings toward my sister have changed. I know your past, and I know you better than you believe, and you would not suit. In fact, your present lifestyle, similar to mine, would indicate you're not suitable for anyone at present."

"That is harsh." Beckett went to disagree but could not. Martin had a point. He had not been looking for a wife, but then, nor had he ever thought to discourage himself from finding one should a desirable woman pass him during the Season.

He ground his teeth, hating that Lady Genevieve had made him feel things he had not for...well, forever. He shook his head, certain it was only because he knew her so well and long that he had such a visceral reaction to her, nothing more. He certainly did not want to court her himself. Nor want her in his bed.

Although one night would be no hardship...
Damn it, man, get a hold of yourself.

"I want your word that you will not court my sister. We've been friends for many years and have been through and experienced much in our lives. I would hate for you to marry Genevieve, knowing what I do about your rakish past. You would only disappoint her, Tyndall. Possibly more so than Venzellons ever could."

Beckett digested the words, unsure he cared for any of them or how it made him look.

"No, Genevieve would be better with Venzellons if it's anyone. I think she would enjoy

New York. She's always wanted to travel, and her life would start with an adventure to the Americas."

"You have my word. I will not court her. I'm merely concerned for Lady Genevieve, that is all. I shall never woo her. Do not be absurd in suggesting such an outcome. But I also cannot agree with Mr. Venzellons being suitable. He's worse than you and I, and Lady Genevieve deserves better than marrying a rogue."

"Well, that is a shame you dislike Mr. Venzellons so."

"And why is that?" Beckett asked.

"Because I invited him to Mama's home tomorrow afternoon, and he assured me he would attend. Will you still make an appearance knowing he's to call?"

Beckett sighed. "Of course. I'm not so much an ass to snub your mama's invitation." Not that it meant he had to be pleasant to the man. That could be a stretch.

CHAPTER
ELEVEN

The afternoon tea held by the Duchess Curzon was well attended. No matter the weather or if anyone felt poorly from the excesses of the night before, few would miss one of the most influential matrons of the *ton's* events.

Lord Tyndall was no exception to this rule either since he'd decided to attend and watch her like her papa had the first time she'd ridden a pony independently.

Genevieve sat beside Matilda. She tapped her slipper against the Abussson rug, waiting for Charlotte to arrive so she could ask what she was doing boating with Tyndall the day before.

Last evening, she had barely slept, so restless at the thought of her friend being courted by such a rogue who, only a few nights ago, was kissing her with abandon.

"I promise you, Genevieve. Charlotte boating with Lord Tyndall meant nothing at all. He was paying her kindness when Lord Wilton, whom she had been walking with in the park, abandoned her to escort Miss Hogsworth boating instead. I swear I did not know where to look at Charlotte's befallen visage, and had you been there, you would have thought highly of Tyndall, as I did that he would save her injured heart at that moment."

Genevieve sighed, wanting to believe Matilda, but she also did not like the unsettled feeling that overcame her at the thought of Tyndall courting another. Perhaps that was why her sleep last night had been far from restful.

Surely not. She loathed Tyndall...

All of her unease, of course, could be laid at Lord Tyndall's door. Had he not kissed her at the Fraser masque, she would not know what it was like to be held in his arms, marked by his wicked lips. The thought of his mouth moving on hers, his tongue utterly inappropriate and delicious against hers, made her skin prickle with awareness even now.

Blasted man.

She looked across the room and met the

very frustrating man's gaze. She ought to look away, but something in his stormy blue eyes meant she could not.

Did not want to.

Oh, please do not be smitten with Tyndall. Of all the men in London, he was the last man she should ever want to marry. They were lifelong enemies—had been for years. After one silly kiss, she could not have feelings—emotions that she had worked so hard to sever—bubble up inside her again and cause strife after his rebuttal of her years ago.

"And anyway, why do you care if Charlotte did romantically like Tyndall? It's not like you want him for yourself. You have your cap set on Mr. Venzellons, who, speaking of the man himself, has just arrived."

As much as she did not want to blast her silly soul, Genevieve looked away from Tyndall and toward Mr. Venzellons, who spoke to her brother and mama. She bestowed a welcoming smile as they made their way across the room to her.

Genevieve stood and patiently waited for Mr. Venzellons to bow before her.

"Genevieve, you remember Mr. Venzellons of New York," her brother said proudly, looking between them both. "Mr. Venzellons, my sister, Lady Genevieve."

Genevieve held out her hand and smiled prettily. Out of her peripheral vision, she could see Tyndall standing nearby, too close for comfort, and his annoyance all but emitting about the room like a burning flame. What was he doing here anyway? He should not interfere in her life, making her uncomfortable at home. Only Mama's friends and gentlemen who wished to court her should be here.

Tyndall had no right to be here at all.

"A pleasure to be reacquainted, Lady Genevieve. At last, I am before one of the most beautiful women London, and I should say England, has to offer." He picked up her gloved hand and kissed it, meeting her eyes as he did so. Not making any mention of them only walking yesterday.

It seemed Mr. Venzellons was fond of games.

"Why thank you," she replied, having heard such compliments many times before. It was disappointing that he could not think of anything more original than all the other gentlemen in town often said to her.

"Would you care to take a stroll, Lady Genevieve? I see others are making use of the gardens this beautiful afternoon."

Well, he may prove a little more interesting after all.

A walk outside, away from her prying family's eyes, was always welcome. "I would like that very much." Genevieve took his arm, and he led her onto the terrace. There was a light breeze this afternoon, but still, the day was warm and comfortable. They walked along the terrace, both quiet for a time, and she wracked her mind for something worthy and interesting to say. For some unknown reason, the silence was awkward, and that did not give her the best reflections for a successful courtship.

"You did not mention that we walked yesterday, Mr. Venzellons. Are you always a little naughty in society that our reintroduction had not occurred earlier?" she couldn't help but ask.

He smirked. "I enjoy playing with words and people, but I promise there is never any malice in my actions." He studied her a moment before he said, "And I'm thankful to your brother for inviting me. I have been deliberating on how to call on you again. I enjoyed our stroll yesterday."

They walked onto a path that led through the lawns and past rows of roses, lavender, rosemary, and foxglove. An abundance of fragrant plants her mama could request the gardener to plant.

"As did I, Mr. Venzellons."

"And now that I have met you and your delightful mama again, I know that I shall wish never to leave." His tone was teasing, his deep American accent thick and low, a huskiness she had not heard before.

"Well, you are most welcome to stay." They passed other couples and groups of friends taking the air before they started back toward the house.

Genevieve glanced toward the terrace. A mistake the moment she did so. Her steps faltered, and she covered her faux pas with a chuckle. "Oh dear, I seemed to have gained a pebble in my slipper. Can we pause here a moment while I fix my shoe?" she asked, uttering a wrinkle. Seeing the angry, disappointed, and tight-lipped Lord Tyndall watching them, she knew Tyndall was no gentleman she wished to encounter too soon.

"Oh, of course, let me help you."

Before Genevieve could protest, Mr. Venzellons kneeled and reached for her foot. He lifted her leg, clasping her thigh. Genevieve gasped, having never been manhandled by a stranger in such a way. The naughty, knowing grin Mr. Venzellons bestowed as he pulled her slipper off her foot and tipped it upside down was one she wasn't sure she liked particularly. It appeared a little menacing, untrustworthy, and the opposite of what he had declared earlier.

"There, it is gone." He slipped her shoe back on, but his hold on her leg lingered for longer than it ought. Heat kissed Genevieve's cheeks, and before she could pull her leg out of his clasp, the shadow of Lord Tyndall covered Mr. Venzellons.

"I suggest you let go of Lady Genevieve's leg before you no longer have hands to hold anything of value ever again." Tyndall's tone was deathly quiet, but to the well-trained ear, one anyone knew not to ignore. Never had she ever heard him sound so incensed and threatening.

A little flutter occurred in her chest. Did Lord Tyndall genuinely care for her reputation... For her?

"And out of curiosity, are you going to be the fellow who removes my hands?" Mr. Venzellons asked, a cocky lift to his lips.

Oh dear, had he truly asked that question?

Genevieve looked around for her brother, her father, anyone to stop what she feared from happening—fisticuffs in her garden before all the *ton*. Her mama would never forgive her for the scandal.

Genevieve stepped between Lord Tyndall and Mr. Venzellons, ensuring no fighting occurred. "I require refreshment, Mr. Venzellons. If you..."

"A wonderful idea, Lady Genevieve. Let me escort you." Tyndall clasped her hand and pulled her away before she could answer.

Mr. Venzellons's startled visage was the last thing she saw before she was towed around the terrace to the side of the house and out of sight of all their guests.

CHAPTER
TWELVE

Lord Tyndall did not speak as he dragged her through the garden and into the conservatory on the opposite side of the house. Genevieve should have stopped him and told his lordship he was taking too many liberties, but she did not. A little wickedness had taken over her soul, and she wanted to see just what his overreaction was about.

He wrenched her to a stop inside the conservatory door and set his hands on his hips. Genevieve stared at him with an innocence she knew would infuriate him further, but she did not care. The man had caused a scene with a gentleman she hoped would prove worthy as her husband. Tyndall was not her brother or father, for that matter. He had no right sticking his perfect nose in her business.

"Is there a reason you're standing before me as if you're about to chastise me for walking about my garden with a gentleman admirer who may end up as my husband?"

"Are you out of your mind, Lady Genevieve? You cannot allow men to clutch at your body as you did. He had hold of your calf, for heaven's sake." Tyndall ran a hand through his hair, leaving it on end.

Without thought, she reached up and fixed a stray loose curl to sit out of his eye.

He clasped her arm. She knew what he had meant to do: push her away, chastise her more, berate her, and remind her of her position and place in society. That she could not let her family down by bringing ruin upon herself, and yet he did not.

He stared at her with a tortured longing that ripped all common sense from her mind. Without care, she closed the space between them, clasped the back of his nape, and kissed him.

She kissed him with all the passion and longing that had built within her over the past years. Let what she had longed for him to do at the tender age of fifteen overwhelm her now.

She'd learned to hate him, yet she also could not stop wanting him in turn.

He growled a deep, tortured sound that

reverberated through her soul, leaving her craving more. He did not pull away, did not push her back, but instead, wrenched her against him and kissed her back. Held her hard against his body.

Genevieve lost all sense of decorum. She wrapped her arms around his neck and kissed him with abandon. His mouth moved, teased, and seduced her into his impure world. She could lose herself there and be happy doing so. Especially when the maddening earl kissed so well as to leave her breathless.

His hands were everywhere. He hoisted her hard against him, and she could feel the hardened outline of his manhood. It ought to frighten her, scare her away, or make her run to her mama and demand she make him marry her, but she did not.

Instead, she settled in to enjoy the delicious pooling of heat between her legs. An ache that, no matter how much she pressed against him, how firm his hand on her bottom was holding her close, would not relent.

"Genevieve, damn it," he moaned, moving them somehow to taunt her more.

Need built to a point that made her senseless. She did not know what it was, but she wanted it with everything that made her who she was. "Tyndall, you make me feel...feel..."

Gosh, she could not catch her breath or form words. The man was discombobulating her utterly.

"Hungry?" he asked, his wicked kiss stealing her breath and what wits she had left.

"So hungry." The word couldn't have fitted the situation better. It was a hunger that only he seemed to evoke and sate simultaneously. And yet, there had to be more to what came after such a kiss, but what? And why did she want Tyndall to be the one to show her...

Everything.

Maddening...

Genevieve felt too right in his arms. He should stop. Quit this madness before they were caught and married before midnight.

He could not.

Never was he so close to losing self-control. Were she not his friend's little sister, he would be tempted to lift up her heavy skirt, stroke her, and sate them both in this humid conservatory.

When the hell had he started to desire Lady Genevieve?

His enemy.

An annoying little minx who followed him around like a lost puppy.

Damn it all to hell. He was the worst of libertines.

With reluctance, he wrenched away and separated them and fought the overwhelming urge to finish what they'd started. "This does *not* change what we were discussing earlier," he managed, his breathless, curt words failing to remove the longing that burned in Genevieve's pretty green eyes. "Your conduct with Mr. Venzellons was inappropriate and courting scandal."

She scoffed and brushed past him, heading toward the conservatory door that led into the main house. "That is rich, my lord. It seems far less scandalous than what we were just doing. Do you know that's the second time you've accosted me? The second time I've felt your manhood straining against your silk breeches." Her gaze dipped to between his legs, and he ground his teeth, knowing what she said was valid and unable to refute it.

"Mr. Venzellons is not suitable for you. I tell you this as a friend. You will be unsatisfied and unhappy in a marriage with him. I doubt he would be faithful." What was he doing? He needed to leave Genevieve alone and allow her to make her own choices, right or wrong. Her family could look out for her and guide her way.

He certainly shouldn't be kissing her in

conservatories and then berating her over her choices, which were none of his business.

"What is going on in here?" Genevieve's brother Martin asked, joining them and looking between them with suspicion.

"Your sister allowed Mr. Venzellons to fix her shoe, and he took liberties by touching her calf. I warned you the man is a scoundrel."

Genevieve scoffed, and he inwardly swore.

Perhaps he was being obstinate, calling Mr. Venzellons a scoundrel, especially when he was one most of the time. Just tonight he had kissed a woman of marriageable age, a virgin, and his friend's sister. He ground his teeth, fisted his hands at his sides, and ignored the ringing in his ears, which refused to relent.

"Genevieve, is that true?" Martin asked, staring at Genevieve.

"I had a pebble in my shoe, and he assisted me. You know how difficult it would have been for me to repair the issue with my gown, brother. Refrain from reading into Lord Tyndall's words. He's overwrought with emotions at present."

Overwrought with emotions?

He glared at her. Did she want to play this game? "Perhaps it is you who has been overwrought by being molested by a man who is not your husband and should return to your room and think upon things and what a young lady as yourself should allow."

Her eyes widened, yet he knew she was intelligent enough to understand that he meant himself and not Venzellons.

"Well, a pebble is nothing, I suppose, and if you say there was nothing untoward occurring, I'm happy not to tell Mama or Papa. But Tyndall is correct. You should retire and rest before this evening. It's been a busy afternoon, and most guests are leaving now, which brings me to why I was looking for you, Tyndall. Would you care for a game of cards at Whites?"

"I would indeed," Beckett replied.

"Come then. I shall order my carriage. You can tie your horse to the back, and we'll travel together."

Beckett watched Martin leave them alone, seemingly forgetting that he ought not.

"Maybe I should tell my brother who else manhandled me this afternoon since you like to snitch, my lord."

He intended to walk past her, leave her alone, and ignore the fire that burned between them, but he could not. He stopped but a breath from her and stared at her beauty, which only increased with each year he knew her.

"If you did that, Genevieve," he said, using

her given name, "we would forever be tied, for you would be my wife. I do not think that is what you want. Not really."

She raised her chin, contemplating his words. "It is not what I envisioned, no. I have thought of a different future for myself, and you must let me try to gain it before you ruin my Season."

"You can choose anyone but him." He hated the idea of her leaving London, England, being so far away...

"That is not your choice," she said, flouncing out of the room as best she could with her voluminous gown.

"Even so, it's not happening," he whispered so she could not hear.

A promise to himself more than anything else. Genevieve would thank him for his intrusion one day. Maybe not today, or this Season, but one day.

CHAPTER
THIRTEEN

Several days later, Beckett received an invitation to attend a dinner hosted by the Duke and Duchess Curzon. An affair that he'd often attended, but agreeing to go, he couldn't help but wonder if there was an alternate reason behind the impromptu dinner.

The duchess didn't usually throw such events through the Season, preferring hosting afternoon tea or her annual ball, but otherwise nothing more.

His carriage pulled up before the grand Georgian home. He adjusted his cravat and checked his attire before a footman ran to the vehicle door to let down the steps and open it for him.

Stepping out of the vehicle, Beckett took a deep breath and looked up at the mansion that had been his second home for many years.

Who else would be here this evening? He could only hope that Mr. Venzellons was not one of them, but something told him he'd be disappointed.

A footman took his greatcoat and led him toward the drawing room where everyone was gathered before the meal. He greeted the duke and duchess, kissing the duchess, whom he saw as a second mother after losing his many years before.

"Tyndall, over here."

Martin's voice caught his attention, and he excused himself and headed over to his friend. "Good evening. Thank you for the invitation."

"Ah yes, well, Genevieve persuaded Mama to host a dinner so she could invite Mr. Venzellons. He's over there speaking to her already. I believe the American wishes to marry her. Can you believe it?"

Tyndall could very well believe it. For all his annoyances when it came to Genevieve, she was uncommonly beautiful and of age.

He took a glass of wine from a passing footman and glanced toward Venzellons and Genevieve.

But he'd be wrong if he expected to see her as he'd always had these past years she'd been out in society, wearing large white wigs with either ribbons or jewels accentuating the opulent pieces.

"I ah..." He couldn't form words. He cleared his throat and sipped his wine, anything to help him function like a human being.

Not since he'd teased her about her hair had he seen it down in its beautiful natural form. But this evening, it sat about her shoulders, long, soft red curls, and a simple ribbon about her crown to hold it away from her face.

His hand shook as he held his glass, unable to tear his eyes from her.

"Stop looking, Tyndall. You'll scare off Venzellons, and no matter what you think, the man is suitable for Genevieve. She's always wanted to travel and see more of the world. A marriage to an American will be good for her. She'll be happy."

She'll be so far away...

He tore his gaze away and fought to look indifferent to the sight of her that still materialized in his mind. Martin suggested they speak to a few of the other ladies present, and Tyndall couldn't agree more.

Anything to keep his mind off what Genevieve looked like this evening. Still, even as he bid good evening to several ladies, one of whom was Lady Matilda, he couldn't keep his attention from snapping back to where Genevieve stood.

She laughed at something Mr. Venzellons said, and Beckett's eyes narrowed. What were they speaking about? Was Venzellons being inappropriate? If the bastard knelt before her and touched her again, he'd not just remove his hands this time but rip his arms off, too.

"Thank you again, Lord Tyndall, for our boating outing in the park the other day. I did enjoy myself."

"Oh," he mumbled, looking away from Genevieve and giving his full attention to Lady Charlotte, who now stood before him. When had she joined their party? Was he so preoccupied with the redhead across the room that he had not noticed? "You're very welcome," he said.

"If you're interested in making me your wife, perhaps we could do it again so you may propose."

"Yes, of course..." Beckett watched Genevieve accept a glass of champagne from Venzellons. Their hands touched, and if he were not mistaken, Genevieve was toying with the gentleman. Flirting.

"Or perhaps you could propose here and now?"

He frowned and turned to Lady Charlotte,

realizing what she was saying—what he'd said. "Oh, I do beg your pardon, Lady Charlotte. I did not mean... I wasn't exactly..."

"Paying attention to what I was conveying?" Lady Charlotte stated matter-of-factly. "Yes, I know, and that is why I said what I did to see if you would respond appropriately." She looked in the direction of her friend. "If you like Genevieve, you should tell her before it is too late."

Beckett took in the advice, unsure if he should say anything to her friend whose loyalty lay with Genevieve and not him. She would likely tell Genevieve everything he said, but that wouldn't do at all.

"We're hardly friends, as you know. I do not look at Lady Genevieve in that way."

Charlotte scoffed, and he faced her. "Please." She rolled her eyes, and Beckett wondered if all young women these days were so bold and forthright in their speech.

The Three Graces certainly seemed to be.

"For a gentleman who's not interested, you certainly seem preoccupied with who's courting her."

"I'm hardly interested. I've merely known her almost all my life and do not want to see her make a mistake."

"Mr. Venzellons will not be a mistake. He's

a rake, like you. Would you be a mistake? Would you treat her poorly if she happened to marry you? Would you continue your lifestyle no matter if you took vows before God?"

"Well, I..." He frowned, the idea of being with anyone other than Genevieve disconcerting. He'd always enjoyed the freedom of being with women who caught his fancy. But recently, when the prospect arose, the women's faces would morph into Genevieve's, leaving him questioning his choices and leaving him even more flummoxed.

What the hell is going on?

He'd never enjoyed her following him around when he was young, and he certainly didn't want her doing the same now. Not that she was, but somehow, in his obsession with her marrying Venzellons, he'd seemed to have traded places with her.

And that was not desirable.

"It's something to think about, is it not?" Lady Charlotte said, watching him over the rim of her champagne glass as she sipped.

Dinner was announced, saving him from having to say anything more. He moved toward the dining room and took his seat, only to find Genevieve seated across from him, Mr. Venzellons at her side—by design, no doubt by the duchess.

He watched them both, picking up his water and sipping. "Lord Tyndall, what a coup being positioned beside you. I have not seen you in some weeks."

He stilled at Lady Masters' seductive tone. Girding his loins, he faced her, smiling. "Good evening. It has been some weeks. How have you been?" He really needed to stop dallying with widowed women of the *ton*. It would certainly save him from awkward conversations such as the one about to proceed.

He glanced across the table and caught Genevieve watching him. The sight of her with her natural hair made the breath catch in his lungs.

Hell, she was utterly divine and looked good enough to eat.

He could not stop admiring her, no matter who watched his lengthy inspection of the duke's daughter.

"I would be better if you called on me, my lord. My kitty misses your pets."

He stilled, hoping no one else heard Lady Masters's words or knew how to interpret them more fully if they did.

However, his hope was dashed the moment he saw Genevieve's scour at her ladyship. Surely Genevieve did not know the meaning behind her ladyship's words. It would be worse if she did. For surely then she understood what had transpired between them in the past.

Shame washed over him before annoyance took its place. "You should amend how you speak, my lady. We're at a dinner, not a private setting," he whispered.

Lady Masters chuckled and made a motion to button her lips before turning to the gentleman to her right.

"Excuse me," he heard Genevieve state.

He looked across to see her gaining her feet before she whispered something to her mother and left the room. Would she return? He wracked his mind with a way to go after her, knowing the possibility was out of the question.

Not without raising suspicions.

He caught Venzellons' smirk as he watched Genevieve leave the room, and everything within him stilled.

Had the man insulted her in some way? Had he been inappropriate?

If he had, there would be an outcome that this American may dislike, and that smirk would be enjoyably wiped off his face by his fist.

CHAPTER
FOURTEEN

There was little chance she was going to return to dinner. The sight of Lord Tyndall and Lady Masters, a known lover of his, was enough to turn anyone's stomach off the roasted Cygnet that her mama was to have served.

And yet, she could not hide out forever in her room. She needed to return and stomach watching Lady Masters fawn over Tyndall as if he were the only man worth having.

He was not. And the sooner the gentleman knew it, the better.

She left her room and returned downstairs, taking her seat beside Mr. Venzellons with an air of nonchalance that was only skin deep.

She could not stand watching another woman remember her night of passion with her enemy—a man who thought too much of himself.

She set her napkin on her lap and reached for her wine.

"I hope all is well, Lady Genevieve?" Mr. Venzellons asked, his kindness unparalleled. She enjoyed his company. He was personable and amusing and always made her laugh.

But something was missing—that spark that she and her friends had often spoken of—chemistry, a hunger that rumbled and grew in size whenever the one gentleman who you did admire was around.

She glanced across the table and met the eyes of Tyndall, who was watching her.

He was trying to figure her out, or at least understand why she had left the table no doubt. He would not be amused if he learned it was because the sight of Lady Masters fawning over him was enough to make her eye twitch.

Why though?

She loathed him—and had done so for years. He was a bully, and he had teased her about her hair, which she had worn down this evening if only to spite him. She had done so, believing that he would look upon her distastefully, just as he had many years before, and her choice would become all the more clear.

And yet, that had not happened.

Quite the opposite in fact. He'd looked taken aback, more enthralled than she'd ever seen him before.

Blasted man needed to work out his mind and feelings.

"All is fine, thank you. I just remembered I'd left my knitting a little too close to the fire in my room."

"Of course," Venzellons replied, clearing his throat. "Have I told you this evening that you look exceptionally beautiful tonight?" He picked up her hand and kissed her gloved fingers.

Genevieve wished the butterflies that continually fluttered in her stomach when she was around Tyndall would do the same for Venzellons, but they did not.

She tried her best to smile, to appear pleased. How disappointing her body was to her. He was so deadly handsome and rich, and he would give her an exciting and different life. And what did she do in return?

Nothing. She felt absolutely nothing at all.

She reached for her wine yet again and Venzellons placed his hand atop hers, stopping her. "Do not gorge too much on the red, Lady Genevieve. You'll be in your cups and unable to hold a proper conversation with me this evening."

She stared at him, waited for him to remove his hand, and then lifted the crystal glass, bringing it to her lips. "I'm parched. I shall drink whenever I choose, Mr. Venzellons." Why on earth was he restricting her so? He'd never been so high-handed before.

"I merely do not wish for our night to be ruined if you're foxed."

"Having a glass or two of wine during dinner will not end in me being foxed." My word, she'd never been foxed in her life and wasn't about to start dallying in the occupation during one of her mother's dinner parties.

"Would you like me to refill your glass?"

Tyndall's deep baritone carried across to her, and she looked at him. He was standing, had procured the red from a footman, and was poised to refill her glass.

"Thank you, yes." She heard Venzellons clear his throat, the tightening of his mouth clearly stating his annoyance Tyndall was supporting her instead of agreeing with him.

"Well, I never thought I'd see the day that an earl would be the footman at a dinner party," Venzellons bellowed, making everyone at the table aware of what Tyndall was doing.

"I never thought I'd see the day that a man of no rank tutored a duke's daughter on how she should behave at a dinner party—one being held by her parents, no less. But perhaps they do things differently in America than here."

"Oh, we do things differently. I can assure you, Lord Tyndall, that no wife of mine would drink in excess, whether at a dinner party of her parents or our own that we're hosting."

"How riveting your dinner parties will be, Mr. Venzellons. Do make sure I'm invited. I'd hate to miss out on all the fun."

"Gentlemen, gentlemen, do enjoy the delicious boiled fowl," her father announced, trying to halt the disagreement between the two dinner guests.

Tyndall finished pouring her glass of wine, before sitting and glaring at Mr. Venzellons.

Venzellons mimicked Tyndall, and a standoff of sorts commenced for a few heartbeats.

Genevieve picked up her wine and took another sip, ignoring the pointed stare emanating from her left.

What on earth had come over Mr. Venzellons this evening, being the way he was? They were not married yet, and he had no right to chastise her or try to halt her from enjoying her mother's delicious claret.

Thankfully, dinner progressed well after this little outburst, and they were soon back in the withdrawing room, enjoying the fire and Lady Poyntz, who played the pianoforte.

Venzellons stood with her father. His gesturing and furrowed brow did not bode well for her papa's enjoyment of his after-dinner drinks.

"I fear your future husband is angry and right now explaining why he is so to your father. Do you think the duke will listen for long or soon bellow the sod away and ask not to be disturbed any longer?"

Genevieve cringed. "I fear from looking at Papa that Mr. Venzellons will soon learn not to displease the duke with his opinions." She turned to Tyndall, reaching up before thinking better of it and clasping his upper arm. "Thank you for pouring me my wine. It saved me from acting like a termagant, which I fear Mr. Venzellons would not approve of. Not for his wife."

"And yet I have heard that he enjoys hellcats in every other aspect of his life. Quite odd, is it not, that he would want his wife to be meek and mild."

"Odd indeed." Genevieve snapped her mouth closed. Why was she agreeing with Tyndall? It would only make him all the more opinionated toward the man she'd chosen to marry.

"I'm glad you've seen sense. I hope this means that you will not marry Mr. Venzellons should he ask."

"Why should I not marry him? Just because he cautioned me on drinking too much wine this evening does not mean he would always do so."

"And if that is what it means, what will you do then? You'll be all the way over in America. We cannot lean across the table then and save your pert ass."

"I never asked you to save my ass, Tyndall."

He narrowed his eyes, glaring at her. "I think your unwillingness to see sense maybe means that you need to be made to see sense."

"Really?" Genevieve turned her nose up in the air, her tone mocking. "And I suppose you're the gentleman to do the teaching."

"I may have to be." He paused. "Have you stopped sneaking out to events not meant for innocent, young, unmarried ladies like yourself?"

"I would not tell you that even if I had. This is my life, and I shall live it as I see fit."

"I will tell your father if you do not cease this madness."

"And I shall tell him how you kissed me,

my lord." She grinned, remembering the feel of his mouth on hers, his tongue, his hands... "Do not forget that we both have secrets we wish to keep hidden."

"You drive me to distraction, Genevieve."

"You forgot to say Lady before my name, my lord. Do not forget again."

CHAPTER
FIFTEEN

Beckett ground his teeth. He was at his wits end with the chit, who was starting to occupy far too much of his deliberations daily.

Mr. Venzellons sauntered about the room, his arrogance enough to make Tyndall's lip curl. Why did he hate the man so much? Was it merely because he was an American in England attempting to steal away a desirable debutante who would suit one of his titled friends? Or was it because the desirable debutante that he had his cap set on was Genevieve?

"Sister," Martin said to Genevieve, who remained beside him. "I've just heard from father that Mr. Venzellons has asked for your hand in marriage. I should think you'll soon have a proposal to enjoy. Are you not happy, sister?"

Genevieve stared at Martin before her attention slipped to Mr. Venzellons, who spoke to Lady Masters. Did she not see that he was in the process of securing another lover? The man was a sad dog and, by the looks of it, had no quibbles about getting what he wanted, even at his future betrothed's dinner party.

"Mr. Venzellons asked Papa for my hand in marriage?"

"Yes, just now. I heard him myself." Martin grinned as if this was the best news. Beckett couldn't think of anything worse than Genevieve leaving to live on the opposite side of the world, possibly never to return to England to visit her friends and family.

You're not her friend. If fact, you've made it perfectly clear that you are the opposite.

All true, and possibly from the uncomfortable feeling in his chest, a truth he would no longer wish to continue.

They disagreed on many things, but he wasn't her enemy. They had once been friends —until he teased her about her red hair.

He could not pull his eyes from the hair that sat about her slim shoulders and voluptuous breasts this evening. When had she become such a beautiful woman—one of the finest in London?

"You look a little stunned, sister. Are you not pleased?" Martin pushed.

"Oh yes, very pleased indeed, and I shall have to think on the matter."

Beckett scoffed. "He's a rogue. Who knows where he's been? I should think the consideration of his offer of marriage would be an easy no to conclude."

"You're no better than Mr. Venzellons if what I know of you is true. Were you not the other day boating with one of my friends? If I were to look up the meaning of the word rake, I would find your name beside it. You cannot place judgment on others when you're not innocent yourself."

"Oh, such fun, but Mama is waving me over to join her," Martin said. "I shall return shortly."

"I do not rut about London," Beckett returned. "And I certainly do not ask for a woman's hand in marriage and then commence caterwauling about town later that same evening."

Genevieve's attention moved to where Mr. Venzellons continued to speak to Lady Masters. Their heads together in quiet discussion, no doubt to ensure privacy.

"We are not married yet. Mr. Venzellons may do as he pleases, but I'm sure you're mistaken. He would not be so cruel as to do what you accuse him of."

"Do you not think?" Beckett did not enjoy being blunt or cruel, especially to a woman, but Genevieve wasn't just any woman. She was his best friend's sister. No matter if they did not always get along, a woman deserved happiness in marriage.

He could not see her accomplishing that with Mr. Venzellons.

"He is not such a rake as you accuse him of. He has not even attempted to kiss me."

Beckett met Genevieve's eyes. Was she referring to their kiss in the conservatory that he had stolen? A kiss that still haunted his bloody dreams and ensured an uncomfortable night's sleep.

"Would you kiss him back if he tried?" Did Beckett want to know this information? He regretted the question the moment he uttered it. He didn't want Genevieve to think that he wanted her forever. That wasn't the case at all. He merely had to look out for her if no one else was seeing the flaws that Mr. Venzellons had ample of.

"I think I would. He appears to be a gentleman who knows how to kiss, and I would so love to be kissed passionately and with great skill."

She did not just say that out loud and to him.

To a man she *had* kissed.

Beckett ground his teeth and concentrated on keeping his breathing steady. He would not rant at her or call her out on her lies, for surely that was what she was doing—taunting him and trying to rile him up.

Was she trying to make him kiss her again?

"Did I not kiss you properly, Lady Genevieve? Is that what you're saying?"

She shrugged, her delicate shoulder catching his eye, not to mention her cleavage. She had all the lovely curves he'd always liked in a woman. When had she blossomed into such a stunning creature?

When he hadn't been looking...

"Yours was a kiss that I've already forgotten. I grant you that the first kiss, when you did not know who I was, was very passionate. But the second was more of a punishment. I felt as if you were telling me off."

"I was."

"I know, that is why I said it."

Beckett cracked his neck, the tension in his shoulders unbearable. The woman was maddening. "Perhaps we ought to try again to see once and for all if I can satisfy your desire for passion."

"Excuse me, my lord, but are you saying we

ought to kiss again here and now?" She grinned mischievously, the teasing minx pouting her lips. "I'm up for it if you are. But then I shall be married to you before the month's out if you continue this tutelage."

"So I'm teaching you now."

"Well, I suppose you have, in a way. Until you, I hadn't kissed anyone, but now I think I know how to. I'm sure Mr. Venzellons will be pleased with my learning, and I do wish to please my husband in all ways, not just kissing."

Beckett cleared his throat, adjusted his cravat, and gestured for a footman to bring over the tray of wine. He needed a drink now. "It's a shame such talents will be wasted on Mr. Venzellons. I doubt he will be as appreciative as he should be."

"Lord Tyndall, what are you trying to say? You seem quite put out that an eligible man is courting me and that I may wish to kiss him one day. You are not jealous, are you, by chance? If you are, why do you not own it and say it out loud."

"What?" he stuttered, hating that she had possibly read him far too well. Was he jealous? Hell, yes, he was. Not because he wanted a wife, but he also hated the idea of Genevieve kissing that lout of a man. Did no one else see that he was an Abram Cove? Surely people were not so blind? "You think too highly of yourself," he answered, hoping it would stop her from reading him anymore. Far too well indeed.

"I think you lie. I think our kiss has shaken you a little off your bachelorhood pedestal, which you enjoy so much. I think you like me more than you're letting on, and the thought of me no longer being available to your beck and call whenever that need may arise has sent you into a panic."

"You are too bold, Lady Genevieve. I do not think that at all. You're my friend's sister. I look at you as I would a sister."

She scoffed, smiling up at him.

Beckett stilled. Such a stunning face, and sweet smile, and a boldness of character that he couldn't help but admire.

Damn it all to hell.

"You did not kiss me like a sister. You kissed me like a lover. Admit it and shame the devil, Lord Tyndall. You want me in your bed, even if you do not wish me as your wife."

And that was the crux of his dilemma, and she had indeed read him well.

"I do not," he lied. "I would never."

She laughed again, the sound mocking as she sauntered away. "I beg to differ."

CHAPTER
SIXTEEN

A night of revelry at Lord and Lady Grey's home was the night's entertainment. Thankfully, this evening, Genevieve's mama had approved the outing, and she was in attendance with the Duchess of Lane-Fox, Lady Matilda's mama, and her elder brother and his fiancée who were recently engaged.

No one could scold her, or order her to return home like an errant child.

Like Lord Tyndall, who, at this moment, watched her over the rim of his whisky glass, his eyes following her around the room, raising one condescending eyebrow whenever he caught her talking or smiling at a gentleman she admired.

This evening, several gentlemen were worthy of conversation, but Mr. Venzellons was her intent. Tonight, she was determined to get an offer of marriage out of the gentleman. He had asked her papa, so it only made sense he would ask her soon after.

Indeed, if she were to flutter her eyelashes and purse her lips, he would see she was interested in his suit and get enough nerve to ask for her hand.

Otherwise, she was unsure what else she had to do to get him to understand that she was open to an offer of marriage.

He asked her father over a week ago, and still, he had not called and proposed his hand —presented a future with him. He must know that her father would have informed her of an imminent offer.

What was wrong with the man?

"Lady Genevieve, may I have the honor of the next dance?"

Genevieve turned, having not seen Mr. Venzellons' approach from behind, even though she'd been looking every which way for his arrival. But never mind, he was here now, inviting her to dance.

"I would like that very much, Mr. Venzellons. Thank you." He led her out onto the dance floor, his hand tight and a little uncomfortable on her arm.

The stirring notes of an allemande started to play, and he pulled her into his arms. He merged skillfully with the other dancers and moved easily around the dance floor.

"You look beautiful this evening, Lady Genevieve." He cleared his throat, taking in those around him before continuing. "There is something that I have been meaning to ask, and I hope now is an appropriate time."

"Of course, you may ask me anything." Was now going to be her moment? Finally, after three Seasons, she was about to become engaged. Oh, how her friends would welcome this news. Be excited for her. Planning a wedding while in the highest echelon of society would be most enjoyable.

He smiled, and Genevieve returned his gesture. Her heart beat fast, and her skin was uncommonly clammy. This was what excitement felt like when one was about to be proposed to. Surely it was...

"I would like to ask if you would honor me to become my wife. I know that my home is far from yours, and it would mean you would leave your beloved England, but I'm more than capable of making you happy. Please consider my request."

Finally, he had proposed, and how did she feel now that he had? Excitement, yes. One being proposed to was always enjoyable, and she had several over the years. But this was the first one she hoped for.

But as thrilling as the proposal was, she felt...*nothing*.

Oh dear. This was not what she had thought to occur, and she did not understand why she was feeling the way she was.

She wanted to be married to him, did she not?

"Mr. Venzellons, I do not know what to say... That is, well, how lovely of you to ask me to be your wife. I had no idea that you saw me in that position."

"Well, of course. I thought I was somewhat bold with my affection for you, but in the future, if you agree with what I wish, I may have to increase my interest so you are aware."

Genevieve used the dance to ponder his question for a heartbeat. Now that he'd asked, did she want to marry him? Become his wife and move to America? At the beginning of the Season nothing more exciting existed in her world, but now, another occupied far too much of her thoughts.

Lord blasted Tyndall...

"May I have a day or two to consider your question, Mr. Venzellons?"

"Oh, please, call me Roger. I do not wish to be so formal with you. In fact..." He spun her to the side of the room, and before Genevieve could say nary a word, he had her in the entrance foyer of the house. "Now, shall we go for a little stroll and get to know each other a little better? Doing so may help you in your decision to become my wife."

She glanced back into the ballroom and noted that no one was watching what she was doing. She would court scandal if she went with Mr. Venzellons, even though he could possibly be her husband very soon.

"I do not think that is wise. It would be best to remain in the ballroom and perhaps dance more."

"Oh no, I've danced enough for one night. I wish to have time alone with you." He walked them along the corridor, past the servants' door to the kitchen downstairs. His arm linked with hers was like a snare.

"I've admired you for a long time, Genevieve, and have often fantasized about kissing your sweet lips."

"My lips?" Genevieve swallowed. While Mr. Venzellons was handsome, she couldn't kiss him even if she'd teased Tyndall about doing so. He'd definitely expect her to marry him then, and maybe he would use their familiarity and force her to wed him.

"We should return, Mr. Venzellons."

He pulled her into a room and closed the door. "No, my sweet. I think it's time for us to become better acquainted. A kiss will do perfectly well. I want to persuade you to marry me if you're in any way doubting your choice."

She *was* doubting her choice. What was wrong with the man, being so bold? Not to mention taking her to a secluded part of the house. Perhaps all her teasing and games were not her best choice, but how to get out of the hazard she was in?

"This is unacceptable, Mr. Venzellons, and you know it is. I ask that you escort me back to the ball before trouble ensues."

"Dearest." He cradled her face, walking her back until her bottom hit the chaise lounge. "Do not play hard to catch now. We're alone and possibly engaged within a few hours. I think the least you could do is kiss me. I will not tell anyone, not even if you do decide against being my wife."

"No, I do not wish to kiss you. I think I must get to know you better before I do such a thing."

"Do not play these games with me. I know you're interested or you would not have allowed me to pursue you these past weeks. Now, kiss me."

He closed the space between them and

kissed her. Genevieve gasped, pressed against his chest, but he would not move. He was like a rock that refused to roll away.

"Mr. Venzellons, stop," she managed to mumble between his forceful kisses. "Stop. I do not want this."

"Of course you want this. Come, kiss me harder." His mouth moved on hers in a punishing way, forcefully taking her mouth to the point of pain.

Genevieve managed to push him away and run for the door, but he caught her voluminous skirt and yanked her to a stop. Her feet slid out from underneath her, and she fell, hitting her mouth on the wood floor.

Pain shot through her teeth and lips, and the taste of blood exploded in her mouth. Panic followed, and Genevieve froze when cool air kissed the backs of her legs.

"Stop. Mr. Venzellons. Stop, please stop."

He did not listen and continued hoisting up her dress.

"Come, my sweet wife-to-be. You'll be mine after tonight, whether you want to be or not."

"No. Stop." Genevieve fought to get up, but he pushed her down, his hand pinning against the back of her neck, squashing her face into the floor.

Tears blurred her vision. This could not be happening to her. How could he do such a cruel, uninvited thing to her person?

"What the fuck is going on in here?"

Beckett's deadly tone boomed through the room, and Mr. Venzellons's weight lifted from her as if he were never there.

CHAPTER
SEVENTEEN

"How dare you interrupt my fiancée and me while we are having an intimate exchange?" Had the situation with Mr. Venzellons not been so horrific, Genevieve would have laughed. But she could not. This was no trivial matter to sweep under an Aubusson rug.

She climbed to her knees, the raised voices of Lord Tyndall and Mr. Venzellons somewhere to her left. Using a small table that sat beside the chaise lounge, she lifted herself up, covering her bottom that Mr. Venzellons had exposed.

Shame washed through her that she'd managed to put herself in such a vulnerable position. Would she be forced to marry him now? She didn't want to be anywhere near him.

She looked at Lord Tyndall and Mr. Venzellons, arguing nose to nose. Her ears were ringing, and it took several moments before she heard their conversation.

"I've compromised her. Lady Genevieve will marry me and no one else."

"The hell she will. I'll see you on a field of honor before I allow her to marry a fortune-hunting, rapist foreigner such as yourself."

Mr. Venzellons scoffed. "You have no choice, Lord Tyndall. If you wanted her for yourself, maybe you should have snuck her away from the ball like I did. I find one must make the most of the situations presented to them, and I could not wait for her to decide to marry me. I've never been a patient man. I take what I want, and now I'll have a duke's daughter as my wife."

Lord Tyndall's fist smacked quickly and hard into Mr. Venzellons's nose. Venzellons stumbled back, but Lord Tyndall wasn't satisfied with that. He followed him to the floor, punching relentlessly into Venzellons's face.

Genevieve stared, unable to move, before she could not stand the sound of bone hitting bone a moment longer.

She reached for Lord Tyndall, trying to pull him off. "Stop, Beckett. Come away. He's not worth your wrath."

"The hell he isn't." Another punch landed on Mr. Venzellons's face, and this time, the man became limp.

Genevieve gasped. "Oh, my," she said, covering her mouth. "You've killed him."

"I haven't killed him." Lord Tyndall stood, wiping his bloodied hand against his coattails. "But I should have." He turned to her, guiding her toward the door. "Come, I'll escort you home. You're not fit to return to the ball. We'll have to sneak out so no one will see you."

She reached up and realized her wig was askew. She tried to straighten it and check her attire, but somehow, between their tussle on the floor, her bodice had ripped, and her corset and shift were showing.

"Oh, Lord Tyndall, I do apologize. I didn't know I was in such disarray."

"Come, we must leave." His lordship escorted her out of the room, taking her through the back gardens and toward the mews. Thankfully, his lordship's carriage was lined up along the road, and he helped her into the vehicle before talking to his driver and giving directions.

The carriage dipped as he stepped into it and came to sit beside her. He pulled her into his arms, and she was glad for her comfort. She tried to clutch her gown together, but there was no use. It was ripped and would need repairing, if possible.

"What happened, Genevieve?"

She frowned, looked out the window, and watched as the streets of Mayfair passed them by. "I do not know. He asked me to go for a stroll, and then the next minute, he was forcing me into that room at the back of the house. I requested he return me to the ball, but he wanted a kiss."

"A kiss? He asked you to kiss him?" Lord Tyndall's voice did not sound right. It shook and was deeper than she had ever heard it before. Was he angry with her for putting herself into such a compromising position? It wouldn't be the first time she had done so this Season.

"You think I brought on what happened to me, do you not? Blame me for wanting Mr. Venzellons to ask me to be his wife."

"I do not blame you at all for what occurred this evening. Mr. Venzellons had no right to touch one inch of your body. Nevertheless, try to kiss you or try other things. I do not know what he would have done had I not found you."

She turned and looked up at Lord Tyndall. Tears made him blurry to look at, and he clasped her jaw, tilting her face up. "Your lip is swollen and cut. Let me see if you've hurt any of your teeth."

She tentatively smiled, and he examined her. "There is no damage to your teeth. Lucky for me, I'm quite fond of your smile."

His eyes widened, and she reached up, pulling his hand from her face and holding it in her lap. "I'm glad. I thought I may have cracked my front tooth when I fell on the floor."

"The bastard ought to be strung up for what he attempted. If I'd been only a minute later."

"I know enough of the opposite sex that, unfortunately, I do know what would have happened had you not found me. Thank you, Beckett. But it doesn't change the fact that if Mr. Venzellons goes to my parents and tells them what's happened, I will be forced to marry him. For all of his horrible actions this evening, he only wants a duke's daughter for his wife. I'll be nothing but a trophy to him, a very wealthy addition to his life. I can see that now."

"Your parents would never force you to marry anyone."

"No, but if he lies and says he did more than you allowed him to, then I will have no choice. They will think there could be a child, and no matter the hurt to me or how much they love me, they will force me to become his wife." Genevieve sniffed. The thought of Mr. Venzellons—after his atrocious actions this evening—becoming her husband made her shiver in disgust.

She reached for Lord Tyndall, clasping the lapels of his coat. "I cannot marry him, Beckett. What am I going to do? I'll be ruined if anyone finds out that we were alone and that I refused his offer of marriage. I'll bring shame to my family. We'll all be ruined. I'll never find a husband, and my parents will ship me off to the country, never to be seen again. I'll..."

"Enough, Genevieve. Stop, you're starting to panic, which will not help anyone. You will not be forced to marry Mr. Venzellons. Over my deceased and decaying body, would I ever allow such an outcome for you."

"Can you speak to my parents? They love you, and they'll listen to you, perhaps more than they will to me. No matter what Mr. Venzellons says. If you tell them the truth and support me, they may allow me to continue on with the Season if Mr. Venzellons does not set out to ruin me."

"I'll not allow him to ruin you. Your parents have been nothing but supportive of me since I lost my own. No matter how often you and I have disagreed, I will not allow that American to have you."

"Thank you, Beckett. My parents will see sense and do what's right."

"Well, of course they will, Genevieve. They will have no choice because I've instructed the driver to head toward Gretna, and we'll be married instead."

"Excuse me?" She fumbled for purchase, unable to comprehend what he was saying. "You cannot marry me. We don't even like each other very much. We argue, and you have a tendency to tell me what to do far too often."

"Your brother is my best friend, and I'll not have his sister ruined, nor will his family name be besmirched. I'll marry you, and then that slimy American can go back to America and stay there."

CHAPTER
EIGHTEEN

Beckett leaned against the squabs and watched as Genevieve slept on the seat across from him. They had managed to pin her gown together with some of her hairpins and removed her wig so she could sleep comfortably as they traveled through the night. Beckett wanted to put enough distance between them and London so no one could catch up.

What he was doing was bold, perhaps not even the right decision. Her family would certainly not like the way he'd gone about saving her reputation.

He tore his gaze away from her, not needing to imagine what could have happened to her or what their marriage would mean. He didn't want Genevieve in a romantic way. He was merely doing her a favor, saving her reputation—nothing more.

The carriage rumbled to a halt before the Pig N' Whistle Inn, their first stop for the night. A young stablehand ran to let down the carriage steps and help Genevieve alight.

A cool drizzle fell about them, and as he joined Genevieve in the inn yard, he took her hand and helped her run toward the inn door. Upon entering the establishment, the noise, merry drinkers, and drunkards who'd imbibed far too much wine before catching their stagecoaches to unknown locations assaulted their ears.

"Ah, Lord Tyndall, good to see you again. I hope you're not after your usual room this evening, my lord. We're heavily booked, I'm afraid."

He inwardly groaned, hating not to have what he was accustomed to, but his stop here was unchartered and not unforeseen. He couldn't expect the inn to accommodate him every time. "We require two rooms, and if the young lady could have a hip bath brought up, we've been traveling for some hours."

"Oh, my lord, we only have one room left." The innkeeper frowned. "Will that suffice?"

"Lord Tyndall. " Genevieve's squeak of

alarm was not unwarranted. "Are you certain you do not have two rooms?" she asked.

The innkeeper checked again. "No, I'm afraid. Only the one, but it is large and at the front of the inn. It enjoys the morning light."

Beckett ground his teeth. He didn't care if it received the morning light or not. What he didn't want to do was sleep next to Genevieve. Even if it were not far from the morning, they would sleep for several hours and possibly continue their journey after luncheon.

"We'll take it if that is all that's available. Thank you."

"Of course, my lord. Right this way."

The innkeeper took them upstairs and deposited them into their room. Genevieve slumped on a chair before the fireplace. A maid, following close on their heels, quickly lit it and left.

"I'll have the bath delivered immediately. Would you like some cheese and bread brought up? Our cook isn't here until the morning for anything more substantial."

"That will do very well. And some wine, thank you."

"Of course." The innkeeper shuffled out of the room, closing the door and leaving them alone. Very much alone.

Genevieve had fallen asleep in the chair, and he watched her for several minutes. Her head slumped in an awkward position, only cushioned by her hands. Even in sleep, Genevieve was a beautiful woman. Perfect brows, full, pink lips that were slightly open in slumber.

The sight of her raised a hunger in him that he'd never had before with anyone. Why it was toward Genevieve, he could not understand. They had been at odds since they were both adolescents. It was his fault they had fallen out. He'd unmercifully teased her regarding her bright-red hair, which was always in disarray and flying all over the place.

There was a time when she looked like a proper hooligan.

How times had changed.

Now... Now all he imagined was running his fingers through her thick, luscious locks. Kiss those lips as much and as often as he liked, and damn if he knew why or what had come over him to warrant that transition.

She was his best friend's little sister. Off-limits. Not his to have.

Still, he wanted her.

Marriage was his only option to save her reputation, but he wouldn't let her know just how much he was under her spell. She would have power over him then and that would never do.

He would protect and save her reputation out of obligation and appreciation for her family and all they had done for him over the years. However, his lifestyle and how he chose to live his life would not be something he would be willing to give up.

The bath and food were delivered, and Genevieve woke, picking at the cheese and drinking the wine with relish. Every so often, her attention would move to the hip bath and the steaming water that sat nearer to the fire than they did.

"How am I supposed to bathe with you in the room?"

Beckett bit back the words that she could bathe very easily, and he'd enjoy every minute of the view, but relented instead. "I'll go down to the taproom, have a beer or two, and return in half an hour. Would that suit you?"

She nodded, and he left her alone, ensuring she locked the door after him.

Instead of going downstairs, he pulled up a chair in the passage and settled beside the door. The sound of her shuffling out of her gown and slipping into the bathwater was torture. He closed his eyes, not hard to imagine what she looked like, naked and wet.

Beckett ran a hand through his hair and took a calming breath. He'd not think about such things. That would only lead to madness.

The sound of her whispered moan had him sitting bolt upright.

What the hell was that?

He put his ear to the door, listening. Surely she wasn't worldly enough to know of self-pleasure? Would she be so bold as to do that in the bath water he'd thought to use next?

He shook the foolhardy thought aside. Who cared about the bath water when he could hear Genevieve pleasuring herself? The urge to lay on the floor and peek under the door or through the keyhole assailed him.

But no, that was no act of a gentleman. And he was a gentleman, even if the little minx inside the room was right at this moment not at all behaving like a lady.

"Oh, Beckett... Yes, touch me."

He swallowed. Hard. His cock went rigid in his breeches, and he sat on the chair, taking deep breaths to calm his overwrought senses.

Her voice was breathless and full of pining. Did she imagine him touching her? Kissing her?

Fucking her?

Surely, she did not know what that entailed. He frowned. He could not imagine her not being a maid. But then, she was a hellion. Had she misbehaved before? Had she experienced desire with another man other than Mr. Venzellons?

No. He shook his head before her high-pitched gasp and satisfied moan tore what little sense he had remaining from his soul.

Never had he heard such a pure, sexual, erotic sound in his life. Even with his lovers, their moans of delight, their gasps for more had never made him want to spend in his pants.

But he could feel the moisture, the pre-come that oozed from his cock.

He looked up and down the passageway and, not seeing anyone, adjusted his dick to a more comfortable position.

Their journey to Gretna would take two days at least at a fast clip, and if this were what he had to endure, she would surely kill him before they reached their destination.

And then they would be married...

He'd have to consummate the marriage.

Bed her.

His mouth dried, and he let out a squeal of alarm when the door was wrenched open. "You can bathe now, Lord Tyndall." Her gaze dipped to his pants, and she chuckled, flouncing to the bed and pulling back the blankets. "I do hope you enjoyed my little performance. I thought it would be amusing to see if you heard me since you refused to give me privacy for my bathing." Her gaze dipped to his rigid cock again, and he slammed the door closed, locking it. "I see that you did. That'll teach you to spy on me."

"I sat out there to ensure your safety," he retorted, defending himself in any way he could, even though he had enjoyed hearing his name on her lips.

"Of course, dearest," she mocked. Goodnight." With those words, she climbed into bed without a by your leave and promptly fell to sleep.

He, on the other hand, did not sleep a wink.

CHAPTER
NINETEEN

Genevieve lay in bed, her back to Lord Tyndall. The sound of him washing himself in the bath was a temptation she fought not to roll over and enjoy.

She could hear what she presumed to be him washing his arms before dipping them under the water to rinse.

To think that in a day or so, he would be her husband was beyond startling. Wanting to be bold and not allow him to believe he knew her as well as he thought, she rolled over and stared at him.

"Will you consummate the marriage with me when we're married?"

His startled gaze met hers across the room, his mouth agape in shock. "Turn about. I'm naked."

She chuckled, not that she could see much

of his person. Only his upper chest and muscled arms. He had a slight feathering of hair across his chest. What would it feel like to run her hands over his body? He seemed far more muscular naked than he did in a superfine coat and waistcoat. Would he be hard under her hand? Did he smell as sweet as his kisses had been?

Well, it wasn't actually sweet. It was sinful, which got her thinking about what would happen once they were joined in holy matrimony.

"You're to be my husband. And I know you've been naked before the fairer sex before. No need to be shy, my lord."

"I do not ask you to turn about for my own vanity, but to spare your blushes. I do not think you're ready to see me in my entirety just yet. I may scare you off. Make you run for the hills and I'll never get to save your reputation then."

"Well, you do speak as if you hide some sort of monster under the water."

"No monster, but what I shield is great enough to scare an innocent maid such as yourself, even if you pretend to be more worldly than you are."

"Oh, you mean when you thought I'd pleasured myself?" She laughed, smiling at him. "Papa has a book in his library that I stole last

Season. Both Charlotte, Matilda, and I have studied it at length. We know a woman can enjoy herself when alone without the help of a husband."

"You may not have done it here this evening, but I'm curious to know if you've done it in the privacy of your own home?"

She had, of course. Why wouldn't she at least see if what was written in a book was truthful or just fanciful text? But while she had sensed a growing, pleasurable sensation, she did not think she enjoyed the explosive conclusion the book said she would.

Not that she would admit such defeat to Lord Tyndall.

"No, of course not. I do not molest myself, my lord. Unlike some in this room, I should imagine."

"You're a liar."

She grinned and continued to watch him. He scrubbed his hair and then dipped under the water, coming back up and shaking off the excess water like a dog.

Water went about the room. Genevieve shook her head. The man was so vexing. Did he know that no matter what he did, he looked attractive doing it?

"And what about you? Do you self-pleasure yourself?"

"All the time."

His honesty brought heat to kiss her cheeks. He stood and faced her, reaching for a towel and showing her without shame his manhood. It was indeed a beasty long thing that hung between his legs. She bit her lip.

That was supposed to enter her?

Something told her that would not at all be comfortable.

"How is that supposed to fit inside me when we're married? I do not like pain, my lord. I'm formidable in many ways, but that only applies to certain situations."

He stepped out of the bath and, with his cloth, dried his manhood but a few steps from the bed. She glanced up, met his eyes, and noted his amused smirk.

"You're enjoying your show, are you not?" she leveled at him.

"There are numerous things I could teach you, Lady Genevieve. It will hurt the first time I enter you. I'll not lie about that. What a shame we're not a love match, and this marriage is only to save your reputation."

"Are you saying that we won't have to sleep with each other than the first consummation?"

"It's probably best. We're hardly friends, and I'm only doing this favor to you out of obligation to your brother and the friendship he's shown me all these years. It's best not to muddy the water, do you not think?"

A tightness settled in her chest, but she nodded, agreeing to his every word. "Of course. I certainly do not wish to rut my nights away with a man who does not find me attractive and never wished to marry me." She smiled, pushing down the hurt his words caused. "We will do well enough, you're right. And I think I'll enjoy not warming your bed. I may go about society like you, enjoy my freedoms."

"Your freedoms? Whatever do you mean?"

She sat up, frowning. "Well, I'll be the Countess Tyndall. Married and able to attend any event I wish without a chaperone. It'll mean I can take my friends with me; all of it will be above board and without scandal. You marrying me relieves many problems I faced as an unmarried maid."

"What problems? From what I could see, you attended balls and parties without chaperoning and have been doing so for months. I was surprised that you'd not fallen into a jam like you did with Venzellons before."

"Either way, I shall enjoy being married to a man who does not wish to warm my bed. I shall be free for the first time in my life."

"My absence from your bed does not mean I'll stand for you warming another's in turn."

"I would not do that. I'm not like you, my lord. I understand the limits of my freedom."

"Well, just so we're in agreement on that." He seized a shirt and slipped it over his head before climbing into bed. He rolled, giving her his back, and she lay on hers, staring at the ceiling.

His warmth seeped across to her, and she turned to watch him sleep.

What a mess this all was. She could only imagine what her family and friends were thinking right now and how much she would have to explain.

But that concern was for another day. First, she needed to live through the consummation, a detail of marriage that she both dreaded and, in turn, could not wait to enjoy.

With Tyndall.

CHAPTER
TWENTY

His cock was as hard as a rock, as hard as it had been the night before when he'd listened to Genevieve pretend to touch herself in the bath. And now, her hand lay low on his stomach, a hand's length from his dick that he would love for her long, slender fingers to wrap around and stroke.

He closed his eyes, breathing deeply, and dared not move.

She lay sprawled against him. Her body wrapped around him like an octopus trying to devour its prey.

Would he like to be eaten by her?

Something told him he would and probably enjoy her mouth with every nibble it bestowed.

His arm lay under her head, and with every

minute that ticked by, it became more and more numb. Damn, she had a heavy head. Maybe it was all that beautiful red, curled hair she possessed.

She mumbled something he could not understand in her sleep and wiggled closer. Her mouth opened with a sigh, her lips tempting him beyond endurance.

This would never do. He couldn't lust after his wife. Not that she was his wife just yet, but she would be... He was only saving her reputation out of duty and friendship.

He would not fall for a pretty face and pleasant body like so many of his friends had in the past.

Genevieve's mouth had always held nothing but spite for him, and no matter his gentlemanly duty, he doubted that would change with the murmuring of a few vows.

Her hand slipped lower onto his cock, and it jumped. She moaned, sliding her leg along his, her mons pressing against his upper thigh and hip. What on earth was she going to do?

Start humping him.

Dear God he wouldn't survive that. He'd likely roll her onto her back, lift her legs about his waist and fuck her like she dreamed he would.

For there was little doubt that was what she was doing right at this moment. She undulated against him, her hand slipping around his cock, curious at first but then determined to see just how hard he could get.

Well, she would not be disappointed. He could get hard as a rock, and should he allow it, she'd come to enjoy his cock as husband and wife. Not that he was going to encourage affection to grow between them. He did not want to love his wife, or for her to love him in return. Even if he could give her a jolly good tumble whenever he wanted.

He did not know how long her ministrations continued, but if she did not stop he would spend all over her hand and the bedding.

But as of yet, there did not seem to be any slowing of her enjoyment. If anything, she seemed to increase her rubbing pace and was close to coming herself.

"Oh, yes, Beckett..."

He bit back a moan. His cock trembled, so deliciously close to coming. He could not stand it a moment longer, he rolled her onto her back, waking her instantly, and pressed his dick against her wet cunny.

Her eyes flew wide, shadowed with desire and sleep.

"What...what are you doing?"

He ground against her, and she half gasped, half moaned. He did it again and saw the moment she came.

Damn, the sound was sweet.

She closed her eyes and threw her head back into the pillow, biting her lip with a determination he could only admire. She didn't want to show him he'd made her climax, shatter her into a million pleasurable pieces with just two strokes of his dick against her flesh.

"Next time you play with me, madam, I'll fuck you until you come, and I'll be joining you on that little conveyance."

"Excuse you?" She wiggled out from beneath him, and he let her go, rolling on his side, and leaning his head on his hand as he watched her fumble about for her clothes.

Not that she had anything other than the opulent ball gown he'd stolen her away from London in.

When she slipped her shift over her body, and picked up her stays she turned, the corset gaping from not being tied.

"I need your help if you please."

"Do you now?" He threw back the bedding, his cock still hard and jutting through his shirt. He ignored her large, shocked eyes that followed his bouncing, engorged dick as he walked toward her.

He stood before her and tried not to laugh. "I guess I can help hold your stays together so you can tie them, even though you've left me hard and unsatisfied. One day remind me to teach you to finish what you've started or someone may term you a tease."

"I never did a thing to you. I don't know what you're talking about."

He laughed. She was lying. He had little doubt she'd remembered her dream that was no dream at all and understood why he'd rubbed her to climax.

"Oh, but you did." Beckett leaned forward and kissed her exposed neck. The scent of jasmine rose from her skin, teasing his senses. There was certainly one thing about Genevieve he could always count on—she always smelled good enough to eat.

"Your clever hand stroked my cock with an experience that leads me to ask if you've ever done such a thing before. I should hope not, however. I would hate to duel with any who claims prior titillation with you."

"Of course I have never done such things, not even with you. You're repulsive, my lord. You ought to be ashamed of yourself."

"Well." He walked over to where his

breeches and boots were and picked up his pants, pulling them on. "I'm not ashamed, merely unsatisfied." He tied his breeches and sat on the wingback chair. "Usually, when a woman plays with my dick, they usually suck it or fuck it, so I suppose you could say I'd love to mix giblets right now. Unlike some others in this room."

"You never did a thing to me. Rubbing yourself against my sex didn't mean anything."

"Really, did it not?" He stood and went to her, closed the space between them. "So you didn't just orgasm, Lady Genevieve. Did I not just make you experience the sweetest pleasure there is on this large, round globe?"

Her face blossomed a pretty pink and he tapped her nose with his finger. "It's okay, wife-to-be. I'll not tell on you and it'll be our secret. But when we're married by tomorrow morning, I am going to take my fill and we'll both enjoy it. After that, once I'm satisfied, we can return to tolerating each other at best."

"Sounds delightful."

He chuckled at the sarcasm that laced her words. "No matter how unsuitable we are regarding our personality, know this. We will do tolerably well in bed when the time comes. I like my women to come first. You'll be no exception."

"Do you always think so highly of yourself?" she asked, slipping on her leather shoes and glaring at him.

"Of course. And you will too, by tomorrow."

CHAPTER
TWENTY-ONE

Thankfully, the next several hours of travel were occupied with them playing cards or sitting in silence—a much preferable way to enjoy Beckett's company than how she had woken up with him hours before.

Not that she hadn't enjoyed the pleasure he'd given her, but it was utterly inappropriate, not to mention high-handed of him.

The man had no shame.

Now, as the carriage rolled through the streets of Gretna, all she could think about was consummating the marriage. Would she enjoy being with him, as a wife is required to be with her husband?

Would it hurt terribly?

Why had she not asked her mama more particulars? A shame none of her friends were married. They would have certainly informed her.

Oh, how they would be curious about what's happened to her. There was little doubt the missive the Beckett sent to London from the inn they stayed at yesterday would have arrived by now.

If they had not already sent out people to find her, her family would know her plans and what she was going to do. They would not be far away, a day at most. But it still gave them time to marry and consummate the marriage, joining them forever, and not even her parents' disappointment or Mr. Venzellons's actions could change her fate.

So long as their marriage stopped Mr. Venzellons from ruining her completely, she was confident that the *ton* would forgive her for running to Gretna to marry.

She was a duke's daughter, after all, and would become a countess after today.

Socially, they would be wise not to cut her.

"Ready, Lady Genevieve?"

Beckett held out his hand for her to take. He stood beside the carriage in front of a blacksmith's workshop. She nodded, clasped his hand, and prepared to marry a man she once adored and now despised.

She frowned, uncertain despised was the right word now...

They went inside, and a woman of middle age greeted them, taking payment from Beckett before they were led farther into the building.

It was only a few minutes, and they stood before the anvil, repeating the vows from the anvil priest, Joseph Paisley, that would tie them together forever.

"I do," she heard Beckett say, his attention on the blacksmith and listening intently to what the man was asking them to repeat.

She glanced around the dirty space. A forge burned bright at the end of the room, warming the space; tools she recognized, a hammer and a punch, sat on a wooden bench, and the air smelled distinctly of horses and smoke.

Her mama would have an apoplexy had she seen where her only daughter had married.

At least she could spare her that ordeal.

The grand wedding the duchess had always wanted Genevieve to have in St George's church would never be now. But in truth, did it matter where one became a wife, so long as they did so legally?

Surely, that was most important.

Although she would have liked to wear a prettier gown than the one she had on, wrinkled and soiled from two days of travel. However, one had to make the most of any situation.

She didn't dare look in a mirror to see her hair's disarray.

"I do," she repeated before the blacksmith pronounced them husband and wife.

And now she was Beckett's wife. Countess Tyndall.

She had hoped it would feel a little more exciting than it did, but all that plagued her was trepidation. Now, he would bed her.

Nerves fluttered in her stomach. He'd been so wild and demanding in the bed yesterday morning. Had thrust against her sex and set her body into a kaleidoscope of pleasure that was different to her private releases.

It had been stronger, more exhilarating, and the sight of Beckett, his eyes wild with need and determination, even now set her heart to race.

"Kiss your beautiful bride, my lord."

Beckett turned to her and smiled before bending and kissing her cheek quickly.

"Thank you, Mr. Paisley, for your services. We're very appreciative."

"You're welcome, and congratulations. May your life be happy and fulfilled."

He led her out into the drizzly rain that had

settled over Gretna. The weather so changeable in Scotland.

"We're to travel to Gretna Hall. We can stable the horses there," Tyndall said to his driver. "We'll stay there for the night and return to London tomorrow."

"Right you are, my lord." The driver tipped his hat, and they climbed into the carriage. Soon, the vehicle lurched forward, and they were on their way.

"Is the accommodation far?" she asked, taking in the small village passing them by.

"It's just up the road." Beckett adjusted his cravat and kept his attention outside the window. As he said, their journey to the hall took minutes only, and soon, they rolled to a stop before a large, white-washed stone building.

Several horses were tied up out front, and two carriages were parked in its courtyard, loaded with luggage. Checking in to their accommodation was simple. Tyndall took care of the particulars of their room, and while doing so, Genevieve glanced into the taproom, where several men and two ladies sat enjoying a light repast.

Had they, too, just married? Or were they yet to say their vows over the anvil?

Her stomach rumbled, and she realized it had been some hours since dinner the night before. They had traveled all night to make Gretna first thing, and she was in dire need of sustenance.

About to ask for food, she heard her new husband order meals, a hip bath, and a fire to be stoked, along with two ladies' gowns for his wife and laundered shifts for her undergarments.

The idea of bathing and dressing in clean clothes sounded heavenly, and if she had not wanted to kiss Tyndall before, she certainly did now.

They were escorted upstairs, and the inn was quite substantial in size and immaculately clean.

The profits from all those who ran away to marry must be substantial indeed.

The room was one of the largest she'd ever been in at an inn, not that she frequented such places often. It housed a large, wooden bed with an abundance of rich green bedding. There was a little table for two to eat their meals, prettily situated near a set of windows that had a view out onto the town.

Genevieve went to the window and noted another couple entering the blacksmiths they'd just departed. She smiled, seeing how happy they were to be marrying each other. She hoped their enthusiasm never ceased.

A maid lit the fire and several lamps before other servants started delivering food, wine, the hip bath, buckets of steaming water, soap, and fresh towels. Before they were finished, two gowns, several years out of fashion were hung in the wardrobe and fresh undergarments were set on the bed.

"Thank you." Tyndall followed the servants to the door, closed and locked it, leaving them alone.

"Behind the privacy screen, there is a little stove that will keep the bath water warm while you bathe. Would you prefer to freshen up first or eat whatever you wish?"

"I shall wash first. I do not feel myself at present."

She approached him and turned, giving him her back. "Could you untie my necklace, my lord? I cannot reach due to the strictures of my gown."

His fingers pressed against her back, and a shiver stole down her spine. His breath teased the hair at the nape of her neck, and she closed her eyes, imagining his clever hands on her in only a few hours.

Would he take her to bed in the afternoon while the day was still present? Or wait until it was dark and seduce her then?

A small smile twisted her lips, and she had

to admit she was looking forward to being a woman and a wife. It was undoubtedly past time that she married, and Tyndall wasn't all bad.

For all his annoying qualities and inability to keep his mouth closed when they were young regarding her hair, he was handsome—well-endowed financially and physically if she were to think so boldly.

He would do well enough.

But would he change for her? Would he be faithful? She did not think he would. He married her out of loyalty to her brother and love for her family, not herself.

He would not want to give up on his wicked lifestyle. The necklace dropped into her hand, and she moved behind the screen, discarding her dress and hoping never to see it again, at least not until it was laundered.

She untied her corsets, thankfully fastened at the front, and slipped her shift off before lowering herself into the steaming water. Picking up the lavender soap, she bathed and washed every part of her body, wanting to remove days of travel.

Admit it, Genevieve, you want to be clean for him.

She would not deny that, either. He, too, would bathe, and maybe their evening would not be so imperfect. At least they would smell nice while doing the marriage act.

Heat kissed her cheeks, and she dipped under the water, wanting to wash her hair. Coming back up, she ran the soap through her hair, scrubbing and washing her scalp.

The soap ran into her eyes, and she dipped it into the water to try to wash it out, but she only spread more soap everywhere.

"Beckett, help," she managed to call. "Can you pass me a cloth? I have soap in my eyes and cannot open them."

She heard his sharp intake of breath before he clasped her hands, giving her a small cloth.

She wiped her eyes and managed to open them enough to see Beckett standing beside the tub, watching her.

The desire that emanated from him sent a flutter of heat to pool at her core. She pretended not to notice and dipped under the water to wash her hair out thoroughly.

"Are you doing that on purpose?" his low, gravelly voice asked.

She wiped her face again with the cloth, glad her hair was rinsed and her eyes were no longer stinging. "Doing what?" she asked innocently.

He kneeled beside the bath, reaching out to trace one of her nipples with his finger. She did not bat his hand away. What was the point? He was her husband now. She was his as much as he was hers.

"You're playing with fire, Countess."

It was the first time he'd called her by her new title, and she liked it. She leaned on the edge of the bath and blinked slowly. "It's a good thing I do not like to be cold, then, my lord."

CHAPTER
TWENTY-TWO

He had a choice to make. Scoop Genevieve out of the bath and claim his newly titled wife. Lay her onto the bed only steps from where he knelt and make her his in the most biblical way.

She certainly seemed open to the idea of consummating the marriage and soon. In fact, she barely looked nervous at all. He'd slept with many women, and he knew when a woman was aroused. Their eyes grew dark with need, their voices lowered, and there was a quickness of breath.

Genevieve had all of those indications, not to mention her rose-pink nipples had puckered.

He licked his lips and debated how this day and night should proceed.

He scooped her out of the bath. She gasped,

and water sloshed onto the floor and over his clothes. He strode a few steps to the bed and laid her upon the crisp, clean sheets.

The sight of her body, naked, her breasts large and full, his to kiss, to lave. He wanted to kiss every inch of her skin, see her writhe with pleasure.

His cock hardened, and he stood beside the bed, untied the two buttons on the front of his shirt, and pulled it over his head.

His breeches proved a little more challenging, especially since they were wet from Genevieve. He tore at the buttons on his falls and wrenched them down, kicking them somewhere near the base of the bed.

Genevieve's eyes went wide as he stood before her and stroked his cock, allowing her to get used to how a man in his full erotic prime appeared.

Her eyes skimmed his body, taking in his every characteristic before settling on his cock.

The sight of her biting her lip, her tongue dipping out to dampen her bottom one, sent his desire to stratospheric levels.

Pull yourself together, man. You're not a green lad who's never slept with a woman before.

She leaned up on her arms, curious about his body and how his cock grew. More than ever at the interest she showed in him.

"May I touch it?"

He swallowed a moan and cursed himself a fool for playing with her the way he had been. He'd thought she would be a little more timid when it came to being with her husband the first time. That he would be in control.

He was well on the way to losing the little amount of authority he possessed.

He inwardly sighed. How typical of Genevieve to see this night as a learning experience and feel a growing need to know everything about it.

"If you wish to." He stepped closer to the bed and let go of his cock. She kneeled before him, and his mind instantly leaped to the imagining of her taking him in her mouth and sucking his rigid staff.

She reached out, her hand cupping the underside of his manhood, her touch unsure and delicate.

He wanted her hands on him, demanding and sure.

He covered her hand with his, guiding her to what he liked. "Clasp it firmly and stoke me. Work me with the palm of your hands and fingers."

She did as he explained, and he closed his eyes, fighting the urge to spend.

"It's like milking a cow, isn't it? I did that

once, you know. It was an odd experience, but I like this better. You're hard. It makes it easier, I find."

He stared at her, nonplussed. "Easier to milk me?"

Her lips twitched. "Yes, in a way." She paused, running a finger over the tip of his cock. "What is this pearl droplet about?"

He groaned, couldn't hold back what the sight of her inspecting, playing with him did to his composure. Wrenched it in two. He didn't want to push her back onto the bed, fuck her until they both shattered into a million pieces like some untamed blaggard, but never had he ever wanted to fuck a woman as bad as he wanted Genevieve right at this moment.

"It's pre-come. When I spend, there will be more of that pearly liquid."

"Really?" Her fingers rolled the droplet between them before she clasped him a second time. "What else can you do with your penis? I know that you'll insert it into me and that it will be painful the first time."

He swallowed, enjoying her touch far more than he should be. "When I do shadow your bedroom door, it'll only be to procure an heir. It shall not be a habitual occasion."

"Of course, I know we're not a love match, and you're doing this out of duty to my family.

You remind me so much that I'm unlikely to forget how we've come to be here."

He ignored her barb and continued. "A woman can take the man's manhood into her mouth and suck him, draw on his cock with her mouth instead of her hand."

"Really?" She stared at his cock, and he blinked. Aware that if she sucked his dick, he'd come.

"No need for you to do that, Genevieve. You're not ready for that yet."

"And if I wanted to try?" She wiggled closer to him on the bed and pulled him nearer with another stroke of his manhood.

Another pearl droplet settled on the end of his cock at the thought of her doing such a thing. With bated breath, he watched as she licked her lips and opened to take him into her mouth.

Fuck me.

His breath seized, and he stilled.

The feel of her lips, her hot mouth circling his cock was exquisite torture. Her tongue guided her way, taking him a little into her mouth at first before she found a rhythm and was soon sucking him with an ability he'd only ever dreamed about.

And those dreams had been erotic and forbidden, and yet, here she was. Administering fellatio, and he was losing his ever-fucking mind.

He ran his fingers through her red, golden hair, fisting some into his hands, guiding her, working himself into her mouth, fucking her.

His balls tightened, and that forever familiar wave of need pooled in his stomach, taunting him that he was close.

"God, yes, Genevieve. Suck my cock." He gasped when she half moaned and half giggled at his command. The sensation rocked through him, teasing him further.

She pulled off, looking up at him from under her long lashes, innocent and his. His breathing ragged, he watched her, clasped her face, and ignored the emotions that overcame him right at that moment.

He couldn't think straight. Couldn't see linear either.

"You taste so good."

"Genevieve." He tumbled them to the bed. She wrapped her legs around his waist, and he couldn't wait. Couldn't be slow or sweet.

He guided himself against her heat. She was wet, so deliciously moist that his mouth watered at the thought of kissing her other sweet lips until she clamped his head between her thighs in pleasure and came on his face.

Beckett thrust into her, taking her innocence and making her his forever. She was tight, and he paused from moving. Instead, he held still and allowed her to adjust to his proportions.

Her breathing was quick, her eyes wide, and she wiggled and tried to move. She was supposed to attempt to make herself more comfortable, not force it too quickly.

"Give yourself a moment. You'll grow used to me being inside you."

She nodded and licked her lips, and he could not deny himself. He kissed her, took her mouth, and devoured her like he'd wanted to from the moment they'd said *I do*.

She kissed him back, and he felt the moment she relaxed and tightened her legs about his back. Her hands against his chest slipped around his neck, and he knew she was ready for more.

And he'd give her what she wanted.

Both of them.

CHAPTER
TWENTY-THREE

The feel of Beckett inside her was peculiar in a warm, inviting, dominating kind of way. While she liked having him there, she was also unused to having another person so close.

Kissing a man was one thing, but consummating a marriage was something entirely different.

She pressed against him, the pain that had seized her at first dissipated, leaving only pleasure, a pleasant sensation that teased the edges of her mind of something that would be extraordinary if she continued.

She reached for him, slipping her arms about his shoulders, and took in the raw, unfiltered visage that was her husband.

His cutting jaw and high cheekbones seemed more angular as he towered over her, pausing to give her time to adjust. He was so handsome, her stomach clenched, and she pulled him closer with her feet, wanting him deeper, harder inside her.

"What are you waiting for?" she teased, knowing that Beckett wouldn't delay this interaction any longer than he had to. She could see by the little blood vessel on his temple that he was fighting against his desire, his need to take her, lay claim.

She could hardly wait.

After all, she was a woman who'd been on the marriage market for some years. Even though she had failed to find a husband before, that did not mean her body had not long craved a man, even though it was only now that she knew what that encompassed.

His mouth twisted into a wicked line, and her breath hitched. He thrust into her, relentless in his taking. His hand reached for hers, forcing them above her head as he pumped with a rhythm that left her breathless.

A tingling, aching sensation teased between her legs. With each stroke, he pushed the growing need to new heights. Was she going to experience another pleasurable experience like the one she'd had with him yesterday at the inn?

Could a woman, when being made love to,

climax this way? How extraordinary and exciting, if that were the case.

His other free hand reached down about her ass, lifting and adjusting the angle of her hip. The change of pitch deepened his reach and, with each relentless, brutal thrust, pressed her ever forward to conclusion.

"Beckett." The beseeching gasp tore from her before she could stop it. "What are you doing to me?"

His eyes met hers as he stroked within her, pressing, teasing, taking her, pushing her to the point of no return. His eyes were dark and stormy with determination and desire.

She could not look away, could not tear herself from watching the emotions and complexities of his face as he gave and took satisfaction from her.

He'd never appeared so deliciously handsome before. That she was here, married to her lifelong nemesis, her bully, and enjoying every little scrumptious thing he was doing to her was madness.

And perhaps she had gone a little wild.

For him...

The thought stilled her mind but a moment before he rolled them over. Somehow, she was now sitting on his lap, staring down at her husband.

His eyes latched on to her breasts before he reached for her, running his hands over her flesh, circling her nipples with his fingers, fascination glowing in his eyes.

"Dear God, you're beautiful."

His words warmed her. How sweet he was. She had not thought he believed her to be anything but an annoying gnat, a pebble in his boot, but perhaps she was not.

Maybe there was hope after all for their marriage that she had failed to see a day or two ago.

"Lift yourself on me. Ride me as if you're trotting on a horse."

For a moment, Genevieve thought about what that movement would entail before she braced herself on his chest and, using her knees, lifted herself upon him.

"Not all the way out, just up and down in short heights."

She did as he instructed, and the sensation was different again. More consuming and satisfying somehow. She came down on him, taking him deep, and gasped, not out of pain, but the bliss that shuddered through her.

"Yes, just like that, little wife."

Wife... She shivered at his endearment. Liking the term more than she ought, especially from Beckett.

She could not comprehend how they were married, here and now, making love. It was utterly bizarre and yet so right. She could not imagine doing what they were with anyone else.

She moved on him with an ease and expertise that she'd not thought she'd have so soon, but it wasn't as difficult as she thought. It was growing more and more enjoyable, her blood warming, her skin prickling with sweat and bliss. Her core ached, and she only built that need with each downward stroke.

She wanted more.

She increased her pace, leaning on him, closed her eyes, and savored the feel of him, hard and thick, filling and inflaming her body.

She moaned, the sound slipping from her lips. "Beckett." She was so close, tittering on the edge, yet could not quite get to where she wanted.

What she now knew him capable of giving her.

He sat up, slipped his arms under hers, and hooked his hands on her shoulders. "Ride me. I'll help you," he said.

She did as he bade, moving on him more forcefully. With his hands gripping her shoulders, his thrust was deep and firm and was all she needed to tip her over that delightful edge that had eluded her thus far.

"Beckett...I'm..." His kiss swallowed her words. His mouth drank her cries as she shattered in his arms. The pleasure too much and yet not enough. She wanted to feel this free again, to float in his arms while locked within his hold.

"Genevieve...I'm coming."

She broke from the kiss. She needed to see him and watch how he came apart. Tremors rocked and thrummed through her as his manhood thickened, hardened more if that were at all possible.

He moaned her name, gasped, and thrust into her as he spent his seed. Warmth flooded between her legs, and she bit her lip, hoping that perhaps, no matter how this union had started, he would not deny her this part of the marriage if he was to deny her everything else.

Love, affection...fidelity.

Worse still, now that she'd had her husband so, longed for more before it had even ended, how was she to live knowing he was to continue his life as before?

Rutting about town as if he were still an unwed man.

They had been enemies before and had

fought too many times to count, but this time, this fight may be one she could not lose.

CHAPTER
TWENTY-FOUR

They sat in the carriage. Several hours had passed since they'd left the last village before entering the outskirts of London. They would return home today and would have to face Genevieve's parents.

Would they be disapproving? Would his lifelong friend call him out and want retribution for stealing his sister away and marrying her?

They had a lot of explanations to give, but when her family knew the truth and the trouble that Genevieve could have been in, they would understand.

They would have to.

His new wife, his in every sense of the word, leaned on her elbow, her chin resting in her hand as she stared out the window at the ever-growing number of houses that lined the road.

Several maids in Gretna had attempted to clean the silk ballgown for Genevieve to return home in, but whatever they'd used to remove the grime had only made the dress appear worse.

Right at this moment, in the lowly dress they had brought up for her to use, she did not represent the duke's daughter she was, or the countess she'd become only two days before.

Still, he could not help but admire how utterly beautiful she was, especially when she did not know she was being watched. Her pretty nose and perfect skin. Her large, green eyes looked upon everything with curiosity and hope.

Her lips... She kissed far better than he'd ever imagined. The memory of them being intimate... His cock twitched, desire twisting in his stomach for more.

With her.

"We'll be home soon. What will you say to Mama and Papa?" she asked.

He shifted on the seat and adjusted his cravat, attempting to tidy his clothing as best he could. "The truth. I will tell them what Mr. Venzellons attempted and what transpired afterward." He shifted his attention to the window also, anything but to be distracted by the sight of his beautiful wife.

A woman he could seduce whenever he wished.

He ground his teeth. He would not seduce her in the carriage only a mile or two from home.

As much as the thought intrigued him.

They traveled in silence the remainder of the way to Mayfair. As instructed, the driver brought the carriage to a halt near the Duke of Curzon's mews, ensuring their arrival back in town was unnoticed by the gossiping *ton*.

He helped Genevieve down from the carriage and, taking her hand, led her through the back garden gate and into the duke's expansive grounds. They ignored the startled, interested glances from several gardeners and were soon striding through the mansion's halls toward the duke's library.

A footman noticed them when they entered the foyer. "Lord Tyndall, the duke has been expecting you. Please do go in."

He frowned and glanced at Genevieve. She squeezed his hand, which he could only assume was in support, and he welcomed her courage. He may need it in the coming minutes.

They entered the duke's library together,

and Genevieve dipped into a curtsy before going to her father and reaching for him.

The duke hugged his daughter, silent, but the relief on His Grace's visage gave Beckett hope that their meeting with him might not be all bad.

"My darling daughter, we have been worried sick." He clasped her by the shoulders and stared at her for several moments. "What happened? We received a hastily written note only from Lord Tyndall and could not make much sense of anything."

"May we be seated?" Beckett asked.

The duke gestured for them to do so, and they sat across from His Grace. "As you know, I attended the same ball as Lady Genevieve several days ago," he started, explaining what had occurred and what he'd stumbled into, and subsequently stopped. But he also noted the damage that Mr. Venzellons seemed determined to do if he did not get his way with Lady Genevieve.

"I could not, you see, allow Lady Genevieve to fall victim to such a man. He was a liar, a cad, and would surely have made her marriage a living nightmare. As her friend and a friend of the family, I would not allow him to mistreat her. I hope you can forgive me for stealing her away. We are married, Your Grace."

The duke showed little emotion, merely stared for some time at them both. Beckett fought not to fidget, to show his unease. Was the duke enraged? Would he demand the marriage be annulled? A little difficult considering they'd consummated it, plus there were other grounds that would make dissolving their marriage impossible.

Still, the duke was a powerful man. He could do anything if he wished it.

"You're married, well, that is some good news, I suppose. As for Mr. Venzellons, he has not caused any trouble in London. In fact, he's already left for India. Wanting a change of atmosphere was his excuse, but I think it was because Martin had words with him one night that he did not particularly enjoy."

Beckett chuckled, liking the idea of Mr. Venzellons getting an uppercut to his jaw. The man deserved no less. "I have the marriage certificate here, Your Grace." He pulled the document out of his pocket and gave it to the duke. "I do apologize for stealing Lady Genevieve from town. But after what I viewed, and given Mr. Venzellons's threats, I thought the best, and quickest way to put his threats to bed was to marry Lady Genevieve myself. She agreed after a little persuading, and here we are."

"Yes, here we all are." The duke's attention

turned to his daughter. "Are you happy with this, my dear? I can always alter this outcome if you're not."

Genevieve was silent for some time. Unease churned in Beckett's stomach before she smiled at her father. "While Lord Tyndall is not the man I thought I would ever marry, it is not so vile that I dislike who is now my husband. We have formed a truce and get along well enough. I think our marriage will be pleasant, and there is little we can do about it now."

"Why, my dear?" the duke asked.

"Well, because we've been intimate, Papa. I could be carrying Lord Tyndall's child as we speak."

Beckett froze at her words. A child. His mind scrambled to think, to plan, to imagine. He'd never spent in a woman before, not without using a French letter. He'd always been so careful. But with Genevieve, he had not been.

But a child?

He wasn't ready to be a father. He wasn't ready to be a husband for that matter.

What had he done?

"Oh, of course. Well, that would be lovely news. For some time, your mama and I had thought you would never marry at all. Since we were unable to attend the event itself, we shall have to host a ball in honor of your nuptials."

"We would love that, Papa."

Genevieve's hand slipped over his, squeezing it and pulling Beckett from the panic that assailed him. He hardly knew how to look after himself, nevertheless another human being. What if he failed and something happened to the babe? To Genevieve? He shivered, the horror not worth thinking of.

"Wouldn't we, my lord?" she asked him.

He nodded, knowing that was what he was supposed to communicate. "Oh, of course. And soon, if you will. Society ought to know our two great families have become one."

He could only hope that it would not increase anymore. Not yet, at least.

CHAPTER
TWENTY-FIVE

"Are you going out, my lord?" Genevieve asked Beckett as he strode past her bedroom door, heading toward the staircase.

He skidded to a stop and stared at her as if he'd forgotten she existed, which wasn't surprising. He'd done exactly that since their return from Gretna this fortnight week.

Ignored her.

Her courses had come, removing any hope she'd harbored of having a child. But now that they had passed, she was desperate to attend a ball as the new Countess Tyndall.

But she could not attend her first event without her husband. What would the *ton* think? Her family and friends? They would all assume that there was trouble already in the marriage, and they would not be wrong.

If he did not touch her soon, she may expire of need.

The man had bewitched her, made such exquisite love to her in Gretna, and then left her out to dry like the linens often hanging on the lines near the mews.

This would never do.

She was a duke's daughter. She wasn't the one to be left home to pretend she was the perfect wife and future mother. Not when her husband refused to be the ideal husband.

"Ah...yes. There's a card game at the club. I'll be seeing your brother and a few friends. I thought we'd make a night of it. It's been some time since I've enjoyed such a night."

She crossed her arms and frowned. "You went out last evening. How long could it have possibly been? Hours?" She paused. "Not to mention you've been out each night since we returned to town. If I were a betting woman, I would say you were purposefully avoiding me."

"I beg your pardon? What are you trying to express?"

"Well, I think I said it quite clearly enough. Are you scared of your wife? We've had our differences, but I thought we'd formed a truce in Scotland."

A muscle worked in his jaw, and his eyes

widened before he started down the hall again. "No time for chatting. I must be off. Have a good evening, dearest."

"Tyndall?" She chased after him, catching him just before the top of the stairs. "Do not dismiss me. Have you lost your mind? This is no way a new wife ought to be treated. I should tell Papa that you're abandoning me."

He walked toward her and clasped her shoulders, a condescending smirk on his lips that she wanted to slap away. "Now, now, wife. Do not be a virago. It's just cards and some wine. Nothing more."

She narrowed her eyes on him. "I do not believe you, and if you think that I'm going to stay at home and be a good little woman for you, you can think again."

It was his turn to cross his arms and glare. "And what do you think you're going to do? Be unfaithful? Beget a bastard in your stomach? I think not."

She gasped, not quite believing he would be so cruel or say something so vile. "Of course not. I'm not some Covent Garden whore. But I do not like being made a fool, and you're making me look like one by not attending the first event together as we should, as society expects."

"You'll have to wait until tomorrow

evening. The Sedgewick ball is then, and it'll be a good time to showcase our delightful marriage."

"Excuse me, what is with the derision in your tone? You're the one who whisked me off to Scotland and married me without a by your leave. I did not ask for you to do that. In fact, I'm certain my father would have protected me from Mr. Venzellons. Why do you not just admit that you like me more than you're willing to concede, and now you're running scared."

There, she had said what she had been thinking these past days.

She had been wondering why he'd avoided her at all costs. It had to be because he did not trust himself around her.

He lusted after her, an emotion she could work to her advantage. Who did not want to make their husbands lust after them? They were wet clay in a woman's hands if she held such control.

He would do what she wished. Instead of going out with his gentleman friends and pretending he was still a bachelor.

"We were barely friends before our marriage. What makes you think that I'm now obsessed with you?"

She stepped up against him and did not

miss the darkening of his gaze or the emotion swirling in his blue eyes when she touched his chest, feathering her fingers over his superfine coat.

She wore nothing but her shift and dressing robe, having been determined to call it a night and remain in her room. His attention dipped to her lips, his mouth opening on a small intake of breath.

He swallowed as she settled her hand on his stomach and felt his corded muscles tighten under her palm.

Oh yes, the man wasn't indifferent, no matter how much he pretended to be.

"When you keep running away, going out every night without your wife, what else is left for me to think? You're scared of me, what I make you feel. While I do not pretend that it's love, you certainly want me. I can see it now, and I would wager that should I touch here," she slipped her hand over his falls and clasped his rigid manhood, taking a moment to stroke him, "yes, there, I rest my case. You remove yourself from this house so I do not tempt you." She laughed and moved away from him. "But I'm not going anywhere, so it'll only be a matter of time before you give up this attempt to remain as you were, and you'll come begging me to forgive you for your obstinance."

He frowned. "You're talking nonsense. That is not what is happening here at all. I'm merely going to Whites to play cards. You're imagining and creating a scenario that is not true."

She shrugged. "Go then, my lord. Enjoy your friends and your whores."

"There are no whores, wife."

Genevieve turned and started back to her room. "I'm certain there are none yet, but there will be. In time, when you've pushed me away too often that I no longer allow you entry into my life, you will seek comfort elsewhere, and then you will regret your choices. But it'll be too late."

"I will attend the Sedgewick ball with you tomorrow evening, and we shall debut our marriage then. This evening is not what you're assuming it is."

"Have a pleasant time at your club, my lord. I shall see you in the morning."

She entered her room and strode directly to her desk, quickly scribbling a note to Charlotte and Matilda. If Lord Tyndall thought to keep her under lock and key, he would think again. She would debut herself as the new Countess Tyndall and allow her husband to explain his absence himself. She was never anyone's fool, and certainly not Beckett's. He ought to be lucky she'd married him at all.

Scandal withstanding or not.

CHAPTER
TWENTY-SIX

Genevieve, Charlotte, and Matilda entered Lord and Lady Bexley's ball later that evening. The event was well on its way to being a crush, with the rooms' gilded walls bursting with the number of people in attendance.

The gowns were opulent, the wine free flowing, the music tempting anyone within hearing of the string quartet.

She greeted the hosts, Lord and Lady Bexley, and proceeded into the ballroom. Many of the guests looked their way, not so much surprised to see her or her friends together, but no doubt her husband's absence would certainly be on the lips of every gossiper come morning.

Which was exactly what she wished.

If Lord Tyndall would not attend the first

ball they had been invited to as a married couple, she would attend on her own.

He would soon come to learn that she did not take well to being slighted, especially by her spouse, nor did she like missing out on balls and parties.

All too soon, they would be returning to the country and leaving London, and they would not be back for several months. Now that she was a wife, she would not get to return to her ancestral home, but have to travel to her new one.

Who knew how boring and dull that home may be? If it was any indication of how her husband was in society these days, it would be dull indeed.

She frowned as they moved through the crowd of guests. In fact, she hardly knew anything about his home in the country. He had always stayed at their estate during school and university breaks. Did he even own one, or was it merely a figment of her imagination?

"You look beautiful this evening, Lady Tyndall," Lady Ashbrook said, dipping into a curtsy. The baron's wife was new to London, having returned after giving birth to their first son last year.

"Thank you, Lady Ashbrook. And you look

well also. Congratulations on the birth of your son. I hear he's charming."

"Oh, he is, thank you, and soon you too will be expecting, I'm sure. Lord Tyndall is a handsome man. I should imagine your marriage is quite passionate."

Genevieve stared at Lady Ashbrook momentarily, her mind blank about what to reply. Was this how married ladies spoke to each other, without any circumspection?

Matilda chuckled and covered her mouth with her fan. "We get along well enough, my lady. Thank you for your kind inquiry." Genevieve moved on, having had enough of that conversation, before they found themselves near the end of the room, watching the *ton* at play.

"An interesting question from Lady Ashbrook and one I'd like to know the answer to as well." Charlotte smirked. "Do tell us, Genevieve, what Lord Tyndall is like in the biblical sense. We're curious to know."

Oh dear, how to answer such a question without turning as red as the rouge she decided not to put on her lips this evening? "I will not lie; he is passionate, or at least, he was when we were married. He has not darkened my door since that day. I'm not sure why."

"Hmm, do you think he regrets marrying you?" Matilda blurted.

Genevieve gasped, unable to believe her friend had said such a thing. Matilda's eyes widened, and she fumbled words, trying to fix her faux pas. "Not so much regret, I amend, but perhaps marrying you has shocked him somehow, and now he's a little spooked."

"Oh yes, I see where you're going with this idea," Charlotte joined in. "Maybe after being with you intimately, he's become a little obsessed, and that's frightened him. Maybe he isn't touching you because if he did, he would lose control of his gentlemanly behavior. The wall that has always been between you both."

Neither were silly notions, and the thought had crossed Genevieve's mind a time or two since returning from Scotland, among other things, that it had been a terrible mistake that she could not undo.

"So what would you suggest I do to try to fix our issues? Seduce him? Deny him? Dress provocatively when in his presence and then deny him? What?"

"All of those things?" Matilda chuckled. "Oh, could you imagine the renowned rake Lord Tyndall falling at your feet begging for you to take mercy on him and allow him to, you know..."

"Sleep with me again?"

"I think she was looking for a more forceful term than sleep."

"I cannot see him doing such a thing," Genevieve stated. "He seems quite determined to keep me at a distance."

"He would be a fool indeed to deny you."

Genevieve hugged Matilda quickly, thankful for her friends with whom she could be herself and say whatever she thought without judgment. "His lordship made it clear in Scotland that this marriage is one of duty for him. He's saved me from ruin from Mr. Venzellons and now thinks his burden is concluded. But not for me. If I'm honest, I find myself a little smitten with my husband. The emotions he made me feel on our first night together... The pleasure I did not know could be gained from another."

"Are you saying what we've learned to do alone is possible with our husbands? I know the book we read said so, but I never truly believed it. Have you seen how many married women walk around London with scowls on their faces and pinched mouths? They do not look like women who've enjoyed their husbands in the marriage bed the night before."

"Charlotte, that is wicked but utterly true. I must agree," Matilda said.

"That is what I'm saying, indeed. While I know we all have explored ourselves in the privacy of our own rooms, I must admit that when Lord Tyndall and I were alone, well, let me just say that the outcome of that union was more forceful, intense, and satisfying than I have ever experienced when by myself."

"Well, that is good news. Maybe I ought to chase Lord Wolfson more forcefully. I want to experience that as well."

"Do not forget me, not that I have found anyone that I like enough to become naked with. Could you imagine?" Charlotte said, her cheeks turning red.

"You're beautiful," Genevieve and Matilda said in unison to Charlotte. "And when you find your husband, he too will fall on his knees and beg for mercy, which is what you deserve and nothing less."

"Well, if our decision is to make Lord Tyndall jealous and raging mad that you're out in society, enjoying balls and parties, wine and good conversation, should you also not enjoy the opposite sex? In a platonic kind of way, but flirt just enough to raise the hackles of Lord Tyndall."

"I think that is exactly what is needed. When one sees the possibility of what they've lost, maybe they will want to win their prize back," Matilda stated.

"Yes, I shall go on as I did before. Enjoy dancing with the gentlemen who pay me notice, and allow Lord Tyndall to learn of his wife's popularity through the members of his precious club."

"Do not forget to taunt him when home as much as you can. If we're to make him realize that you're the only woman he needs and should ravish, then he must see what he's missing and for what, a Covent Garden whore."

The idea made Genevieve's stomach twist. Could she be so bold? Push her husband and see how far she needed to go before he folds to her bidding. To her affection?

"Let us hope he's not reverting to his old ways, merely keeping a distance from me because of the stipulations we discussed above. Pray for me that he'll not be able to deny me forever, that his lust for me will grow into love."

"Do you love him? Have you fallen in love with your husband?" Matilda asked, her eyes wide with shock.

"I do not know what I feel for Beckett, but I know it's muddled and as confusing as I think he is feeling right now. I would like a love match, as we all would. Whether I get that outcome is yet to be seen, but I shall not give up without a fight—even if that fight is a little seedy and beneath the actions of a lady."

"When has being a lady ever got us far? I say play dirty and win, especially if that prize is love," Charlotte said.

"Hear, hear," Matilda agreed.

Genevieve nodded. Let the games begin.

CHAPTER
TWENTY-SEVEN

The night was late. Beckett glanced at the clock on the study wall. Three in the morning. A chill descended in the air, and he rose from the settee to throw another log on the fire. He stood, staring at the flames, contemplating where the hell his wife was.

She had been prepared for bed when he'd left earlier tonight. The image of her nightdress was burned into his mind and had taunted him at Whites.

The clock struck the quarter hour. Surely she would not be much longer. Not that it was overly late for those enjoying the Season. Events often ran until dawn, but still, he'd thought she was home, asleep in her bed.

Safe.

When he'd checked in on her upon his arrival home, he'd been surprised to find her bed turned down by her maid, a candle alight on the mantel, but no Genevieve to speak of. He'd returned downstairs and ordered a light repast before settling in to see how long it would be before his wife returned.

Hours had passed since then, and along with it, his patience.

That she was out made no sense at all. They had agreed to attend the Sedgewick ball together. Their first as a married couple. Why had she decided to attend another on her own?

The sound of the front door closing snapped him out of his musings. The light, slippered footsteps had him striding toward the library door to catch Genevieve before she headed upstairs.

He stepped out into the foyer just as she caught her foot on the bottom stair, tripping forward and landing on her hands. A little drunken chuckle escaped her, and he frowned.

Was she foxed?

"What are you doing, Lady Tyndall?" He stepped out into the foyer and got a better look at her. Her wig was askew, her gown creased from a night of revelry, and her cheeks were rosy from fatigue.

What had she been up to?

He took a calming breath, unwilling to

imagine possibilities that were untrue. That would only lead to anxiety and arguments, not to mention make him lose the little control he had left when it came to his wife.

"I was at the Bexley ball. Do not be so daft as to not know where I was, my lord."

"I thought we agreed not to attend any event until I was free to escort you as your husband."

"Well—" She stumbled off the staircase and landed against him. He helped her stand up straight, and she patted his chest condescendingly. He ground his teeth. She was foxed and utterly legless. He would be surprised if she could remember anything they discussed or what she got up to this evening.

Which seemed to be far more excitement than he had. The card game had been dull, and the women who had promenaded about them uninspiring, each looking to be a kept woman. He'd found he wasn't interested in their wiles, no matter how much they tried. A vexing change that he couldn't understand.

In the end, he'd come home early, only to find the house empty and his wife missing.

"You should have agreed to come with me instead of attending your precious card game." She laughed, pushed past him, and started for the library. He followed, finding her before the fire warming her hands. "It's not like I do not know what occurs at those card games. While I know we've not been married long, I had hoped you would not bring back the pox so soon into our marriage bed."

The pox?

He gaped and fumbled for the right words to respond. "Are you insinuating that I tumbled another woman into bed this evening?"

She shrugged, appearing not the least concerned that may be true. The idea was not to be borne, and Beckett wasn't entirely comfortable with how annoyed that made him feel.

He glowered. "Madam, I asked you a question."

"Oh dear, did you ask me a question? Well, I best answer before you're put out with me." She snorted and then fell into a giggle of laughs. "Is it not true? I do not know if you remember, my lord husband, but I have a brother. And I'm more than aware from his drunken self returning home from such events that you attended this evening and what occurs at them." She stared at him, appearing all of a sudden quite sober. "Can you deny it? Were there ladies present or not this evening? Did anyone sit on your lap, hoping for an enjoyable ride?"

Beckett cleared his throat, having never

been asked such a question before. "Stop being a haranguing wife. It doesn't become you." He started for the door but could hear her following close on his boots.

She pulled at his arm, turning him about. "Were there women at your card game this evening? It's a simple enough question. Why will you not answer it?"

"Because it does not signify if they were there or not."

She crossed her arms, raising her already ample bosom higher against her bodice. He fought not to ogle. He truly did, but she was a beautiful woman.

His woman.

His wife.

He ground his teeth, ran a hand through his hair, and wondered how he could escape and get out of this conversation before another word was spoken.

"Answer the question, and don't be such a coward, Tyndall."

Coward? He narrowed his eyes, closed the space between them, and towered over her. "Of course, there were women present. Beautiful women. Women that would get on their knees and pleasure me if I only asked."

A muscle worked in her jaw, and a pang of regret ran through him that he'd hit a nerve.

She did not deserve to be treated thus, not by him or anyone else. Genevieve had done nothing wrong. Their marriage had been his choice, his decision.

"Well, where I went this evening, there were men. Many gentlemen eager to meet the newly married Lady Tyndall." She twirled before him, arms outstretched. "I danced all night and even received a request or two for a stroll in the gardens. I was very flattered."

"And did you agree to their request?" A knot of anger boiled up in his stomach. It was not an emotion he was used to feeling. Had gentlemen, some of them possibly his friends, asked her on a midnight stroll? Their interest was clear, and he knew what they'd been after. A stolen kiss, perhaps more if she allowed. She was married, after all. Fair game to those men who did not care who she was, so long as they did not have to marry her and she was safe to dally with.

He knew the men well.

He was one of them.

Well, *had* been one of them.

"Not yet, but the Season has not ended. There is still time." She pushed past him, and he clasped her arm, pulling her against him. She gasped, her breasts pressing against his chest, her face tilted up to look at him. He could so easily lean down and kiss her sweet mouth. Teach her how she could go on her knees and do what he craved. Teach her that if anyone was going to kiss her tonight, it would be him and only him.

"Do not make a fool of me, wife. I'll not take kindly to it."

"Oh, will you not? Well, nor should I if you rut about London without a care. If I should die because you could not keep your manhood out of another woman's body, I will cut it off before I'm laid to rest. Be assured of that, my lord."

"And if you cuckold me and carry another man's child, pretending for it to be mine, I shall... I shall..."

"What? There will be no proof of my infidelity. However, I'm certain we'll all know if you have the pox or some other infliction."

He stared at her, unsure how this conversation had degraded to the point that they were threatening each other. The idea of her, her body growing to accommodate a child that was not his, made him want to cast up his accounts.

"I shall send you to the country to live out your days there. Alone."

She laughed, turned on her heel, and started for the door. "Well, I'm certain there will be men somewhere out in the country to keep me company, especially if my husband will not."

He gaped, watched as she flounced out the door without a care. She would not dare do such a horrible thing to him. She was playing with him, nothing more.

Surely she was.

Wasn't she?

CHAPTER
TWENTY-EIGHT

Over the next week, they went to several balls and two dinners, one hosted in their honor. Her new husband was the epitome of a gentleman. He helped her upstairs, smiled and flattered her at every turn, and watched her lovingly across the room, yet she knew it was all a front. He was playing with her, attempting to right what he'd done wrong the week before.

The blaggard not only hinted there were ladies present at his card game but taunted her by not telling her what had happened. She did not need him to remind her of the ladies' wiles or their trade. She clutched her glass harder, hating the jealousy that burned through her at the thought of his disloyalty.

Lord Lennox joined her, handing her a fresh glass of champagne. Tonight, they were at her parents' grand London estate and enjoying their wedding ball, which her mama had painstakingly organized in record time just to ensure the *ton* accepted her marriage to Tyndall and no harm was done to her name due to the Gretna marriage.

Her poor mama really needed to stop worrying about what everyone thought. Her mother was the Duchess of Curzon. They only cared what she thought and would be guided by her in all ways.

Mr. Venzellons was of no consequence.

"Thank you," she said, smiling at the tall earl with striking blue eyes and blond hair that flopped over one eye. To be sure, he was a handsome man, but still, blast it all to Hades, not as attractive as her husband.

She darted a look across the room and found Beckett standing with Charlotte and Matilda, watching her. Even when he sipped the disgusting whisky he enjoyed so much, his gaze never left her.

What was the man thinking? He probably thought she was going to walk out in the gardens with Lord Lennox and allow him to have his way with her like some hussy with no morals.

Not that it wasn't tempting to see what Beckett would do should they move out onto the terrace. The doors to outside were just behind her, it would be so easy to suggest...

"I suppose I should congratulate you on your marriage, Lady Tyndall, although for us poor souls, it's a sad loss indeed to society. Whatever shall we do when all three of The Graces are married?"

She laughed, possibly more pronounced than necessary. He'd not said anything overly amusing, but her husband did not know that. She let him stand across the room, glowering at her and wondering what she was talking about with this handsome young man.

And he was younger than Beckett, that was certain, closer to her in age than her husband.

"Despair not, my lord. I still have two friends who remain unmarried and are very much on the marriage mart."

His lordship glanced to where Charlotte and Matilda stood, now talking to each other. Her husband somehow squeezed between the pair. Could he not move? The sight brought a smirk to her lips.

"Ah, but did I not mention that I prefer redheads? I've heard a rumor that your hair under that elaborate, jewel-encrusted wig is that color beneath. Am I mistaken in that dream? Please do not tell me if I'm wrong. It shall shatter my illusions."

She bit her lip, heat blossoming on her cheek. "I cannot tell you that, my lord. That would be very personal, and only my parents' closest friends and myself know the truth."

"And no doubt your husband. I should imagine seeing you with your hair down would be quite the sight. I'm very much green with envy."

"A shame to be sure, Lord Lennox," Beckett said, startling Genevieve, who had not seen him move across the room to join them.

He took her hand, slipped it over his arm, and patted it, but in truth, he was keeping her lodged firmly at his side and in his hold. "If you wished for Lady Tyndall to become Lady Lennox, you ought to have asked her. She had been a thrice debuting debutante."

"I was not a thrice debutante. You can only debut once," she interjected, not liking Beckett referring to her as some recurring desperate woman seeking the affections of the opposite sex. Her friends and she had purposefully not married, and she had turned down many marriage proposals because none of them were suitable. None were love matches.

And still, she seemed to have married a man who was her enemy, not the love of her life.

Fool.

"Even so, if you should excuse us. I wish to have a word with my *wife*." Beckett accentuated the word wife, and had it been a knife, it would surely have nicked Lord Lennox's chin.

They moved through the ballroom and into the foyer before Beckett started upstairs.

"Where are you going?" she asked, trying to pull him to a stop.

"Where is your room? We need to have a conversation."

She raised her brow, chuckling at his annoyed tone. "Really? What about?"

They made the top landing, and he looked left and right, debating which way they should go. Genevieve remained quiet, waiting for him to lose his patience and ask.

"Well, where is your room?"

"Left, my lord. Sixth door on your left."

He pulled her down the hall. Only a few sconces on the wall were alight in this part of the house. They entered her room, still the same as when she left it the night they had traveled to Scotland. Her mama not quite ready to admit that her daughter was now married and no longer living under her roof.

"Are you purposefully trying to cause another scandal? Lord Lennox was asking you about your hair. And you were taunting him, teasing him as if you're not already married to me."

"Well, are we married? You certainly do not act like it."

"And what do you mean by that?" He crossed his arms, glaring down at her.

She swallowed, hating that even when terribly angry with him, she was also terribly attracted to the man. It had been days and days since they'd been together intimately. A week at least, and her body craved him.

She would taunt him in any way she could to provoke a reaction from the beast. She may not like her husband, but she certainly lusted after the fellow. God help her wicked soul.

"We do not share meals or time alone after balls and parties. You do not share my bed. I feel like I'm living in some shared accommodation like an inn or finishing school. Tell me, because I'm certain it would be similar to how you lived at Eton all those years ago."

"Except when I lived with my fellow classmates at Eton, we were friends."

His words stung, and she bit her tongue to stop the tears that threatened. "If you seek and receive pleasure elsewhere, then so shall I. I will not die a shriveled-up woman of a lord who would not pleasure his wife."

She pushed past him, and he hauled her

around the stomach. Her back pressed against his chest, and his breath tickled the whorl of her ear.

"You would not dare seek pleasure elsewhere."

"Would I not?" she taunted, turning her head a little to look back at him.

What she witnessed was wild, untamed, and too far gone to haul back, rein in, and control. Had she pushed Beckett too far?

His hand slipped over her breast, and he squeezed her flesh through her elaborate corset. Where there should be pain, only pleasure shot through her body, directly to her core. She squirmed, pressed into his hold, wanting more like some wanton.

Who was she when around him? She did not recognize herself.

"You're mine, Genevieve." His hand slid down her stomach to press the sensitive flesh between her legs through the yards and yards of cloth. Even so, she felt his touch as if there were no barriers between them.

She moaned, giving way to how he made her feel.

"Do you want me to prove my point?"

Did she? Her body ached and craved his touch. The release she had come to dream of could be but an answer away. She nodded, undulating in his hold as his hand stroked between her thighs.

"Do your worst, my lord. I doubt you have it in you to make me scream."

He chuckled, the sound full of dark determination. "We'll see about that."

CHAPTER
TWENTY-NINE

Beckett wasn't sure what came over him. Pride? Determination? Lust for his wife?

He wouldn't think about how it had made him feel seeing her talking, laughing, flirting with Lord Lennox. The man was stepping across a line, and he would have a word or several with the young earl before the week was out.

He scooped Genevieve into his arms and strode to her bed, tossing her onto the top of the coverings. He enjoyed the sight of the shock and expectation that burned in her green gaze.

She lay back, supported on her elbows, watching him. "And now that you have me here, what will you do to me, husband?"

Was she taunting him? Hunger burned

deep within him, and he wanted to teach her a lesson about heckling a man—her husband—and what he might do to her.

There were so many things he'd fantasized about doing. Tonight, right now, would merely be one.

He wrenched off his coat and waistcoat and threw them over a nearby settee. His cravat followed. For what he had planned, he needed only a little freedom for movement.

He reached for the hem of her dress, sliding it up her slim legs. She wore silk stockings with pretty little pink ribbons about her upper thighs. He stepped between her legs, pushing her knees apart and giving him a full view of the pink, wet quim that was his to enjoy.

She was ready for him, and he could see that she expected him to make love to her.

And while he would take his fill, right here and now was all about teaching her a lesson on who owned her body and soul, who could tease and twist her desire for him for his own needs.

She was his, and by the end of tonight, she would never doubt that or want anyone else.

"Lie back and try not to scream, if you can."

"You think highly of yourself yet again. I do not know why I continue to be amused by your highhandedness."

"You'll see soon enough." He crawled onto the bed, kissed along her silk stocking, lifting one leg and licking behind one knee. She giggled and gasped when he playfully nipped the flesh along her upper thigh, making his way toward her delicious sex.

He could smell her desire, it made his mouth salivate, and he licked his lips, eager to taste her, fuck her in all senses of the word... with his tongue.

He settled between her legs and used his tongue to tease her. She tasted divine, and a hungry growl escaped him before he could stop it.

His hard cock pressed against the bed. He wanted her desperately, but right now, he needed this more. Needed to show her how he could make her feel. Show her the heights only he would bring her now that they were married.

Her legs fell lax, giving him room to enjoy her. He loved on her sex, suckled her little engorged nubbin, and kissed her sweet lips until she was writhing on the bed.

"Beckett."

The sound of his name, a cry, a moan of delight almost made him spend in his breeches. He slipped a finger into her warm, tight heat, and she moaned, her fingers clasping his hair, fisting it tight.

"Fuck my face, Genevieve. Take your fill. Come for me."

"What are you doing to me?" Her breathless plea was music to his ears.

He continued, relentlessly teasing her honeyed flesh. She undulated against his mouth, pressed down on his hand, fucked him as he asked.

"Beckett!" she screamed his name as her body convulsed about his finger. He laved her wanton flesh as she rode out her orgasm, wanting her right to the very end, not leaving her in the least unsatisfied by his touch.

With one last kiss on her mons, he went to move off the bed, but as quick as a flash, Genevieve moved, pushing him onto the bedding to straddle him.

"Where are you going?" she asked.

He stared at her, unable to comprehend what she was doing or how she'd maneuvered him so effortlessly.

She reached for the falls of his breeches, ripping them open. His cock sprang free, hard as hell and unsatisfied.

He was in a great tweague, certain his cods would explode.

She clasped his cock, guiding him into her.

The abundance of her gown made it hard for him to see what she was doing, but by God, he could feel it.

He slipped into her tight, wet heat. So good. So fucking tight. He swallowed and fought to control his emotions and needs.

She did not give him time to catch his breath. She rose and lowered herself on him, working him with a madness that stole the breath in his lungs.

She was magnificent. He drank her in, she appeared just as she would in a ballroom, beautifully dressed, wig perfectly coiffured, a gown fit for a queen, and yet, in this room, hidden beneath yards of material that bustled up around them both, she fucked him like one of the best courtesans in Europe.

He would never survive.

His balls tightened, his cock hardened. He clasped her hips, thrust into her, needing to come as much as his body needed air.

She gasped, rolled her hips, and took him deep.

Her second orgasm convulsed about his cock, and it was too much. He couldn't hold back, couldn't delay the exquisite pleasure a moment longer.

"Genevieve," he gasped, rocking into her, taking her, filling her with his seed. He came hard and fast, the pleasure making stars twinkle before his eyes.

"Beckett, yes, oh yes." She worked him, squeezing every last tremor from them both.

His breathing ragged, he watched her in awe of what she'd done. He'd not expected her to take command. He'd thought she would have been satisfied and left their earlier interaction at that.

To ensure he, too, gained release was an act he'd not expected.

She wiggled off his lap and slumped on the bed at his side. Without thought, he pulled her into his arms as he tried to regain his equilibrium.

Genevieve snuggled into his side, her hand idly lying across his chest. He frowned, unsure what was happening here or why he liked having her in his arms.

They had not been friends, not for years. Their marriage was out of duty and that friendship for her family.

Why was he lying here, holding her, wanting her in his arms, protected and safe?

She kissed his chest through his shirt and sat up before shuffling to the side of the bed. The moment she moved away, he missed her already.

His frown deepened.

"Thank you for the pleasant interlude, husband. I shall never think of my room the same way again. See you at home."

With those words, she turned on her slippered heel and left the room.

Beckett sat up, gaped at the closing door, and swore.

She left him here?

Had he just been used? For sex? For relief?

Well, he never... Certainly, he'd always been the one to leave a lover after an interlude, never the woman.

But it would seem yet again his wife was a conundrum. A minx.

A woman he could not make out.

What would he do with her now?

CHAPTER
THIRTY

The following morning, Genevieve sat down at the breakfast table, her steaming pot of tea, lightly toasted bread, and ham set out before her. Her appetite this morning was indeed considerable, and she could only put it down to last evening's endeavors with her husband.

Their wedding ball, held by her dear parents, had been a success, and no one dared mention that the marriage itself happened in Scotland.

And what had occurred in her bedroom had been an added boon she'd not thought to experience. Since their marriage, Beckett had barely looked at her, nevertheless touched her.

Not that she particularly wanted him to. Well, she wouldn't have prior to their marriage. They were barely friends, but after what he made her feel, how was one now to go about life and not enjoy such interludes?

If he did not wish to darken her bedroom door, he should not have shown her another side of marriage to begin with. Her desire, which was what it was when all was said and done, was his fault. Her wanting him, at least continually, could all be laid at his feet.

A footman set down the latest paper, and she glanced at it, not in the mood for more serious matters pertaining to London and England in general.

"Can you advise me when Lord Tyndall returns from his club? I wish to speak with him."

"Lord Tyndall, my lady?" The footman stood to attention and stared at her as if she had suddenly sprouted two heads.

"Yes, Lord Tyndall, can you give him a message that I wish to see him when he returns home?" She poured herself a second cup of tea, picked up her knife, and spread some jam onto her toast.

The footman cleared his throat. "His lordship, my lady, is asleep in his library this morning. He returned not long after you last evening, but we found him resting downstairs. We have not disturbed him."

The knife fell out of her hold and clattered

onto the plate. She picked it up, finishing spreading her jam before taking a bite and digesting both her breakfast and what the footman had said.

"Are you certain his lordship arrived home early last evening?" That was odd of Beckett, who found his club his second home these past weeks.

"Yes, my lady. I'm most certain. His lordship arrives home most evenings only a little after yourself, but remains downstairs."

She placed down her toast and stared at the footman, a little astonished at this announcement. Beckett returned home not long after she did. She had been having nightmares of where he'd been going at all hours of the night, what ladies were trying to cozy up to him, what he was doing with those who wooed him with their wiles.

And all the while, he was under the very roof she lay beneath, except hiding in the library.

"Thank you. I shall seek out his lordship after I break my fast."

"Yes, my lady."

Determined not to rush, she took her time finishing her meal and even spent a good ten minutes reading the newspaper, or at least pretending to, before she pushed back her chair and went in search of Beckett.

She was supposed to attend a ball at Vauxhall Pleasure Gardens this evening. The invitation had been for both of them, but Beckett hadn't mentioned it in passing these past days.

She might consider bringing Matilda and Charlotte if he were not attending, even though the ball was rumored to be for married couples only.

She knocked on the library door, but when she received no response, she turned the handle and entered where Beckett was hiding these days.

No light penetrated the room, and the shutters and curtains remained closed. The fire had long burned to nothing but a few glowing coals.

She shut the door and walked over to the settee. Beckett lay on his back, his head cushioned by one arm, the other falling to the side, his fingers just grazing the Aubusson rug.

A shadow of stubble sat on his chiseled jaw, his mouth open a little in sleep.

She could not help but stare at his beauty. This virile, handsome rogue was her husband. A boy she had once adored and grew to hate after his teasing of her.

She reached up, feeling her red curls, free to

do as they pleased in the privacy of her own home. But how could she know for certain that there may be a possibility for them? A true connection that went past the physical compatibility they shared? There was little doubt that he found her attractive and wanted her in his bed when he allowed himself to admit such things, even if he'd never outwardly confess it.

But she couldn't help but feel the inklings of those old dormant feelings she had quashed for so long, pretending that those emotions had been twisted into contempt and annoyance. For when standing before him now, watching him sleep, she knew those emotions to be quite the opposite.

She still loved him as much as she had when she was an impressionable girl, with nothing but hope and expectation in her eyes whenever she was around him.

He'd been older, much wiser, she believed, and how she adored him. The way he spoke, so clear and confident, rode horses like he'd been born to live in a saddle or swam in her family's lake during his time with them at the estate was perfect.

Until he'd taunted her and broken her young heart.

She frowned, trying to remember his exact words.

At the tender age of fifteen, she'd been devastated by his teasing, but maybe that was all it was. He was jovial and did not mean to cause such an offense.

She sat on the settee and touched his chest, shaking him a little. "Beckett, are you going to get up today or slouch in your library until this evening?"

He mumbled something she did not catch under his breath and clasped her hand, holding it firmly against his chest. His heart beat against her palm. He was warm, wore nothing but his shirt and breeches, and his feet were uncovered.

He'd obviously attempted to undress and had stopped halfway.

He startled awake, his attention snapping to where his hand pressed hers against his chest. His eyes met hers, and he let go, attempting to sit up and ignore the fact that he'd been holding her hand close to his heart.

"What time is it?" He rubbed his face with his hands, blinking.

"It's just after ten in the morning, but I wanted to come and ask you if you'll attend the Vauxhall ball this evening. The invitation states that married couples are preferred, and I want to go, but I cannot without you. I could try to sneak Matilda and Charlotte in, but I would not need to if you go with me."

"The Vauxhall ball?" He paused, frowning. "I cannot, I'm afraid. A previous engagement, you understand."

Annoyance settled in her chest, and she fought not to glower. "What previous event? It will look crass if I attend the ball without you. People will think there is something amiss in our marriage."

He scoffed and stood, moving over to the bellpull and ringing for a servant. "Well, isn't there something amiss? Need I remind you we're not a love match? We're merely a match made due to my gentlemanly behavior and unwillingness to see my best friend's family ruined."

She swallowed, confused after their interlude last night where she'd thought—hoped—they may have a new arrangement. But apparently not. Yet again, he was pushing her away, keeping her at arm's length. "Very well." She stood and started for the door. "You've made yourself perfectly clear. Have a good day."

She stormed out into the hall, probably less ladylike than a countess ought to be, but the man was maddening. How could he be so sweet, so determined to show her she was his, only to push her away the next day?

Well, if he would not attend with her, she would simply go on her own. And if he would not commit and wanted to continue with his life, then so too would she.

Two could play at his cat and mouse game, and she'd learned many years ago that she grew claws when wronged, and maybe it was time Beckett was scratched.

CHAPTER
THIRTY-ONE

Perhaps it was misguided of her to attend the Vauxhall ball, but when her vexing husband refused to accompany her to an event she was desperate to attend, one had to make one's own decisions.

The carriage rocked to a halt before the gates of the pleasure gardens, and she could already hear the orchestra playing, the laughter that carried through the still night to all those rushing to attend.

"Please remain here, Jeffries. I shall return later in the evening."

Her carriage driver dipped his hat. "Of course, my lady." He cleared his throat. "Are you certain you do not wish for me to escort you? Vauxhall isn't always safe."

Genevieve waved his concerns aside. "I have friends who are in attendance. All will be well." She left him to find a place to park the carriage and started into the gardens.

People milled about her, and she held her head high and hoped what she'd said was true, that she would at least find a friend or two at the ball. Lord and Lady Ramsbury's Vauxhall ball was held yearly, and although she wasn't close to her ladyship, they were of a similar age. Except Lady Ramsbury had married her first Season, while Genevieve had not.

She strolled around the outdoor ballroom and watched the dancers for several minutes before Lord Lennox stood at her side, smiling down at her with his handsome face.

"You came, Lady Tyndall." He looked around as if searching for someone, her husband, she could only assume. Well, he would be hard-pressed to find Tyndall since he'd decided not to attend.

"Where is Lord Tyndall? Tell me he hasn't allowed you to attend this ball without his protection."

She smiled at him, but inwardly, she seethed that Beckett had refused. The man was up and down, and she never knew which way he was going to land on any given day.

Some days, he was possessive, almost loving, and acted the opposite of those who marry out of duty or arrangement. But other times, he was cold, aloof, and uncaring.

Vexing...

"He had other commitments, unfortunately."

"Or, fortunately for me and others I'm certain. We will ensure you're safe and enjoy your night."

"We?" she queried, interested in who the *we* were.

"Lord and Lady Ramsbury and myself, of course."

She smiled, relieved it wasn't some other gentleman she hardly knew. "Well then, this evening will be a triumph. Shall we dance?" she boldly asked.

"Yes, let us." He pulled her onto the dance floor. The music lifted her spirits, even if she annoyingly wished there was another gentleman in her arms, spinning her about the ballroom floor right at this moment.

If only the feelings she had suppressed all those years ago would not have reawakened now that she was married to Beckett. Life would be much easier if she did not care for him. Far too much not to be hurt each time he pushed her away.

She threw herself into the dance, lost herself in the music, and set out to enjoy her night in the arms of another man.

Beckett looked up from the game of Faro as Genevieve's brother stormed across the room, his face set in a thunderous manner.

"What are you doing here?" Martin asked, pulling a chair beside the card table and joining him and Lord Morton.

"I'm playing Faro. Why do you think I'm here?" he answered.

Lord Morton chuckled and played a hand.

"Leave, Morton. I need to speak to my brother-in-law in private."

"Is it urgent?" Beckett asked, frowning and not particularly liking his friend's tone or the demands on others.

"It is of the utmost urgency."

Morton sighed and pushed out of his chair. "We'll continue when your conversation is at an end."

"Thank you," Beckett said, turning back to Martin. "What is all this about? Why are you here all discombobulated?"

"Because my sister, your wife, need I remind you, is at the Vauxhall ball. Alone."

"Genevieve attended Lord and Lady Ramsbury's ball?" A knot of fear, mixed with anger, settled in his stomach. "I told her not to attend. I explained only yesterday that I had another commitment and could not escort her. I assumed she would, therefore, send her apologies." He pushed away from the table, forgetting about finishing the game. "Did she take a chaperone?"

"No one. I received word from a good friend that Lord Lennox is quite taken with her and is enjoying their time, following her skirts about, if you understand my words. If you do not wish for all of London to believe your wife is intimate with another man, I suggest you forget these trivial gambling nights and go fetch her."

"She's not a wolfhound, Martin. I cannot fetch her, but I will go and make an appearance. Ensure that her actions do not ruin her."

"Yes, and perhaps you both ought to stop these games and admit to what is really happening between you both. You're both so stubbornly...stubborn. Can you not see that you're both madly in love with each other but refuse to admit the truth? Have been so for years."

"What?" The breath in Beckett's lungs seized at the word love. He was not in love with his wife. Martin was absurd, had possibly lost his damn mind. He did not love his wife. He barely liked her.

The thought shamed him, and he had to admit that thinking in such a way was not true. He did like her, far more than he'd ever thought he would. They had been at odds for so many years, back and forth with insults and social cuts, that it almost became second nature to aggravate her at every turn.

But now, married to her, loving her when they were alone...well, he could not deny that she made him feel things he'd never thought to ever experience with anyone.

That it was Genevieve was a realization he didn't want to admit to. To do so would give her power over him, and he hated not being in control of his life. After his parents' death, he'd lost all control of his upbringing, his schooling, who tended his estates, everything. It became ingrained in him when he reached age to never let anyone tell him what to do or how to do anything in his life. To love and lose that he loved was a hurt he could not survive a second time. The loss of his parents had been hard enough.

Genevieve included in the people he kept at arm's length, not allowing her to grow too close to him to take his power.

"You both pretend to detest each other, but it's not true. Genevieve has loved you since I first introduced you at our country estate. And since your marriage, I've seen you at the events you attend together. You watch her like a hawk. You lust after her as much as you admire her. But let me tell you something, you should not deny what you both clearly feel. What a life wasted if you both continue to play this stupid game of who hates the other the most when it's clear you love each other equally." Martin paused as they strode out of the house to where his carriage was parked. "Other men see your distance, and I know you do not wish to have anyone close to you for fear of losing them as you lost your parents. But others will give her what she needs, affection, praise, and attention, and you will lose her. Of course, you can never divorce, but a rift will grow between you that can never be breached. I do not want that for either of you. So please, go to Vauxhall and tell her how you feel. Admit it to yourself that you love her, red hair and all."

CHAPTER
THIRTY-TWO

Within the hour, his carriage had arrived at Vauxhall. He walked around the crowds, speaking to those he recognized, yet his wife remained frustratingly aloof.

Fear bundled in his stomach that perhaps she had found herself at the hands of unsavory gentlemen or had left with Lord Lennox. He would kill him stone dead if the earl dared touch one hair on his wife's head.

Surely, she would not be so foolish as to leave with a man, not her husband, or walk the gardens alone. No, she would be well and safe, and nothing would happen to her.

He would never forgive himself if she came to some harm, and he refused to escort her as he ought to have when she asked.

He shook his head, walked through the

bustling crowds, checked every supper box, and spoke to several friends, all of whom said they had seen Lady Tyndall earlier in the night, but not for some time since.

Had she walked off into the gardens with some unknown gentleman admirer? She would not have done such an underhanded, cruel act toward him, surely.

They were married, and although they may not have always been close, surely she would know that he had not been unfaithful these past weeks and expected the same from her.

A familiar sight of red, flaming hair caught his eye, and he pushed through the crowd, only to come upon the revelers and find that it was not Genevieve at all.

Not that she would not have worn a wig this evening. She only wore her hair down in private.

Where was she?

Lord Lennox caught his eye across the grounds and started toward him. Beckett hated that the man seemed a little uneasy and uncomfortable in his presence. Had he taken liberties that were not his to enjoy? He would see him at dawn if he had.

Beckett's eye twitched. "Lord Lennox, I hope you're enjoying your night."

The young buck chuckled and lifted his

whisky in salute. "Always, but it doesn't appear as if you are. Is there something amiss, Lord Tyndall. You seemed a little flustered. Have you lost something?"

He narrowed his eyes on the young man, not appreciating that he would call him out so. Yes, he was unsettled, he couldn't find his damn wife, and this little popinjay had followed her skirts for some weeks, and no doubt knew if Genevieve was still here.

"Where is she?" he asked bluntly. Not bothering to name Genevieve. Lord Lennox knew of whom he spoke.

He shrugged. "I do not know. We parted ways some hours ago." He tapped his chin. "Oh, that is right, I remember now. She mentioned another ball in Mayfair, a masquerade, or was it a costume ball. I forget now. There are so many held each night it is hard to keep up."

Beckett ignored his vagueness and fought not to throttle the truth out of him. "Are you saying Lady Tyndall has left?"

"I think so, but should you not know where your wife is, my lord? That is bad form, I must say."

Beckett didn't bother to answer. He merely turned on his heel and started back to where his carriage was parked. He would attend every ball and dinner this evening in town if it meant finding where his wife was.

Not that he cared that she enjoyed society. She was a duke's daughter, she was brought up to rule over society, be the matriarch for the rich, but he didn't like not knowing exactly where she was.

The Vauxhall ball was a seedy, dangerous place, and if she had left, which surely she had as he could not find her, was a little comfort to his nerves.

But he needed to find her. Ensure she was well and safe.

Confirm she was still his and no one else's.

"Mayfair, Tommy, and quickly, man," he ordered his driver, climbing into the carriage and slamming the door closed. The carriage lurched forward as his driver did as he was instructed.

They moved toward Mayfair at a good clip and it wasn't long before they were back in town.

He jumped from the vehicle before it stopped before the Fraser town house, the very one where he'd shared the first kiss with Genevieve.

Was she here, masquerading and flirting with other gentlemen who offered her the attention and affection she craved but he had not given her?

He ought to be shot for pushing her away as long as he had. Was Martin correct? Did he love his wife? Was the fear of losing anyone he cared for ever again keeping him from giving her his heart?

He'd lost his parents, two good people he missed every day, even now. Was he subconsciously keeping Genevieve at a distance in case something dreadful happened to her, too?

Panic crawled over his skin, and he pushed it down, not wanting it to shadow his judgment. All would be well. She would be at one of these events, no doubt with her friends.

He entered the house, shrouded with shadows, music, and people doing nefarious things in secluded corners. He walked around, looking for anyone who appeared similar to Genevieve. A difficult assignment since everyone was cloaked or wearing masks.

"Lord Tyndall, I did not think you would be here this evening? Lady Masters is over there," Lady Fraser suggested, nodding in the direction of a previous lover.

He smiled, not wanting to be rude, even though a set down that she would suggest he be unfaithful to his wife sat on the tip of his tongue. "I wondered if Lady Tyndall has arrived? We thought to attend this evening."

"Oh, the countess? No, I have not seen her, but be sure to enjoy your time here until she arrives." Lady Fraser flounced off, and he wanted to cast up his accounts.

Did they all believe him to be the type of man who would be unfaithful? Of course, they did. He'd taunted Genevieve that he would not change, but that was far from the truth. He had changed. She had changed him.

For the better, no less.

He left the masque and, over the next several hours, visited entertainments of all levels of society, but Genevieve was still nowhere to be found.

Where the hell was she?

He stood at the Haddington ball, ran a hand through his hair, and spied Lady Charlotte and Matilda. Hope shot through him, and he started toward them. Where The Graces were, typically Genevieve was also.

"Lord Tyndall, how good to see you." Lady Matilda looked past him, eagerness in her gaze. "Where is Genevieve? We hoped to see her this evening, even though she said she had another engagement."

"So she's not here?" He swallowed the terror and tried to look nonchalant, but it was not good. He had checked all over London, and she was nowhere to be found.

Was she hurt, lying on some cobbled road, or cold, dark walk at Vauxhall injured?

"No, she was to attend the Vauxhall ball, but we could not go. It was a little too scandalous for unmarried women such as ourselves, but she said you were joining her and could not make this event."

He nodded, his mind racing. Sweat broke out on his skin, and his legs felt suddenly weak.

"I must go." He wished he could remove the fear that his words brought on Genevieve's friends' faces, but he did not have the time.

He ran from the ball, climbing into his carriage and calling it to return home. He would change his clothing, gather his staff, steward, and everyone if need be, and start searching all over London.

If Genevieve was in trouble, he would find and save her before it was too late.

Only minutes later, he arrived home. He bolted from the carriage, shouting orders no sooner had he entered the house. He ran up the stairs and met his valet in the passage, carrying several clothing items downstairs.

"Steven, help me change. I cannot find Lady Tyndall, and I fear something untoward has occurred this evening. I need your help." He entered his room, ripping off his cravat and hearing his valet follow close on his heels.

"My lord, if I may..."

"I've looked at every ball and party in London this evening, and she is nowhere to be found. I need our biggest, burly footmen to search the grounds at Vauxhall. I shall supply the vehicle and send my man of business to gather help from as many London watchmen as we can hire. We must find her."

"My lord."

"Send word to her ladyship's father, the duke. He will assist me in finding her."

"Lord Tyndall, allow me to speak a moment," his valet almost yelled.

Beckett looked up from pulling off his evening shoes to replace them with riding boots. "What is it, man? We must act with haste."

"My lord, Lady Tyndall is asleep in her room. She's been home for hours, returned but an hour or two after leaving this evening for the Vauxhall ball. There is no need to send out a search party, for her ladyship is safely ensconced next door."

CHAPTER
THIRTY-THREE

Genevieve woke up with a start when a hand pressed against her leg and weight settled beside her on the bed.

She sat up, blinking in an attempt to clear her vision. "Beckett, what..." She wiggled up to lean against the headboard and tried to focus on him in the shadowed room. "What are you doing here? You scared me."

He ran a hand through his hair and sighed, the sound rich with relief. "I ah...there is something we need to speak about."

Fear settled in her stomach, and she clutched her abdomen. Had he done something he should not have? Had he finally found comfort in the arms of another, a notion that she had been dreading the moment he said their marriage was nothing but a duty?

"What is it?" She watched him, braced herself for the injury that would come, the blow against her heart. "Has something happened?"

He reached for the candle at the side of the bed, quickly walked to the fire, and lit it before returning, giving them light.

She could see him now; he looked ragged and tired, and a shadow of newly grown stubble darkened his handsome jaw.

Instinctively, she touched his cheek, hoping he wasn't about to break her heart.

"Your brother came to Whites this evening, demanding that I go and collect you from the Vauxhall Ball. He said it wasn't appropriate you were there alone, and others had made mention of it. I thought we agreed that you would not attend, so I was surprised to hear you were present."

She narrowed her eyes, not wishing to have another argument regarding what social events she attended, but something was wrong. Something told her Beckett wasn't himself right at this moment.

"I did ask you to accompany me, and you refused. If you wish to continue attending different social events, then yes, there will be ones I attend that you may not like."

"Genevieve, it was dangerous, and when I went to Vauxhall..."

"You attended the ball at Vauxhall? I did not see you there."

"Well, no, I could not find you either, and I panicked. I searched everywhere, returned to Mayfair, and I think I attended every social event in London this evening. I'm certain I looked like a madman, but I was frantic. I thought something had happened to you. Your friends did not know where you were, and upon returning home, about to gather the staff to start searching for you, I was informed you were in bed all along."

She should not have, but her lips twitched at his searching for her. Did this mean that he cared for her? That he wasn't so immune to affection, and dare she hope, love?

An emotion that she could no longer deny herself. She adored him. In truth, no matter how maddening he was, she had never stopped loving him, from her childhood infatuation, even during their sparring years, to their marriage.

She loved him and could not deny that truth.

"Vauxhall was of little entertainment value, and I returned home after only an hour or so of arriving there. I'm sorry I worried you so much."

He nodded but continued to look troubled.

"And that is what else I wished to speak to you about."

"You do?"

He rubbed a hand over his jaw, meeting her eye. "I realized something this evening that I've been denying myself. For weeks, I've been aloof, distant, attempting to continue my life as before we were married."

"You've laid with another woman?" The thought made her want to retch.

He frowned, shaking his head. "God, no, not that. I have not had the desire to sleep with anyone other than you, and that is what I'm getting at, Genevieve."

She swallowed the tiny flicker of hope that sparked within her. Was she not alone in her feelings for the man before her? "Go on," she said, anticipation taking hold of her heart.

"You know I lost my parents when I was young, and your brother, my friend, offered me his family to guide and support me and take me in on holidays and Christmas. I'll be forever grateful to the duke and duchess." He paused, rubbing his hands down his pant legs, his fingers shaking with nerves. "But that is not why I married you, even if I stated as much."

She remained quiet, digesting his words and trying to control her beating heart. "Why did you marry me if not out of duty, Beckett?"

He watched her, his eyes burning with fear and, dare she think it, love. "Because somehow, some time since our first kiss at the masquerade, I've fallen in love with you. The thought of you marrying anyone else repulsed and drove a fear so deep in me that I could not see straight. I followed you that night with Mr. Venzellons not out of chance, but because there was no way in hell that I would allow him to marry you. Take you away from England, from your home, from me."

"Oh, Beckett..."

He wrenched from the bed and paced beside it. She followed him. "I've feared loving again after my parents died, and then tonight, when I could not find you anywhere, that fear took hold twofold, made me crazed, and I regretted everything. I regretted not telling you I loved you. That you're everything I ever wanted and did not know I needed. The thought that I could lose you too, that you were hurt, injured, come to be the victim of unsavory men, was enough to make me lose my mind."

She stared at him, unable to believe what he was saying, but so grateful he was being honest.

Finally.

"I never wanted to feel again the loss I had

when my parents died. By loving you, I would open myself up to experiencing that loss again should anything happen to you. But after tonight, I realized that loving you, adoring and being with you, and giving you my heart far outweighs any fear I harbor. I would rather love you to the best of my ability than live without love or affection for the rest of my life. That is no life at all."

Without saying a word, Genevieve pulled Beckett into a tight embrace. She held him and ran her hand over his back, attempting to settle the fear that coursed through him still.

The muscles under her hands were tense, and she could feel his heart beating quickly against hers.

"I'm sorry you worried so, but truly, I'm fine. But I promise I shall not attend another event such as Vauxhall ball without you being by my side."

"I will not let you out of my sight." He half-heartedly laughed, holding her tight.

"Beckett?" she asked, looking up at him.

"Yes?" He stared down at her, uncertain and vulnerable. More so than she'd ever seen him before in her life.

"I love you too."

He smirked at her words and hoisted her into his arms. "You do?"

"I never stopped, and that is the truth. I love you, too. As maddening as I find you, I cannot help myself."

He chuckled and walked them over to the bed. They collapsed onto the bedding, their legs tangling, her heart full of adoration and desire.

"I also have a confession."

"Another one? You are busy this evening." She laughed, slipping her hands over his shoulders and pulling him close. His kiss was soft, and her body yearned for release. "What is it?" she asked.

He stared down at her, their gazes locked. "I've always loved your fiery, red hair. I know I teased and hurt your feelings, but it was only because I needed to keep you at arm's length. I did not want to admit that even when we were children, I thought you were the prettiest girl I'd ever met."

Genevieve bit her lip, her vision of him blurring with tears. "You've always loved my red hair? I do not believe it."

"Believe it," he said, kissing her again. He reached for her nightdress, and she helped him wiggle it over her hips and off her body. He kneeled, quickly stripping off his waistcoat and shirt, his breeches following close on their heels. They came together in a maddening, desperate way she'd never felt before.

He thrust into her, taking her, making her his, owning every part of her soul. She gave it up to him, to the love they had and the life they would enjoy.

"Genevieve, you're so beautiful. I love you," he whispered against her lips.

She kissed him back, locked her feet behind his back, and took him deep. Loving him both in body and soul. "I love you too."

They came together, hard and fast, the intoxicating, convulsing of their bodies in unison all that she ever wanted. So right, so perfect.

"Beckett." His name came out as a plea, a promise to be his forever.

But then, she'd always been his. She merely had to wait for him to realize that he'd always been hers, too.

"How am I ever to keep my hands off of you now? I'm a doomed rake."

She grinned, running her hands through his hair, drinking in the sight of his handsome face, her husband's beautiful charm that took her breath away. "Who said anything about keeping our hands off each other? We're married. We can do whatever we like, when and wherever we wish."

He growled, his manhood thickening again

inside her. "You're very naughty, Lady Tyndall."

"You have no idea," she teased, rolling him onto his back and showing him just how naughty she could be.

EPILOGUE

Genevieve and Beckett were welcomed into the Duke D'Estel's London estate, which was as grand as her father's. They were ushered into the sitting room, which overlooked the grand terrace.

Lady Charlotte greeted them as the footman announced their arrival and came over and kissed Genevieve's cheek in welcome. "Thank you for coming today. I'm sorry I could not attend your small dinner the other week. I'm still terribly sore, I'm afraid."

"How is your finger?" They sat, and Genevieve reached out to look at Charlotte's finger, which she had broken after falling off her horse in Hyde Park three weeks before.

"Unfortunately, I'm terribly sore, and I find it difficult to hold cutlery, so a dinner party would not have been a good outcome. But the splint is helping, and I hope in three more weeks it will be healed, and I shall be able to return to the Season and finish it off with you and Matilda."

"I hope so, too," Genevieve said. Beckett reached out, clasped her hand, and placed it on his lap.

Charlotte smiled at their linked fingers and raised her brow. "And what was the dinner in celebration of? Matilda would not tell me, said you wished to inform me yourself, even though I tried terribly hard to get the truth out of her."

Genevieve laughed, remembering telling Matilda that if she told Charlotte before she had the chance, she would not be welcomed to any future shooting parties at their country estate. A pastime that Matilda enjoyed most when at her family's home in the county.

"Well, we wished to tell you, face to face, that I'm going to have a baby. The doctor confirmed it last week, and we're due before the next Season, so I may be back in London with you all next year. But we'll have to see."

Charlotte's eyes flew wide before she jumped up and pulled Genevieve into a fierce hug. "Oh, my dearest friend. A baby and a husband in the same year. I'm so happy for you, for you both."

"Thank you," Beckett said, standing and

kissing Charlotte on the cheek before she burst into a flood of tears. "Now, now, none of that. This is good news," he said, patting her shoulder.

"I know, but I'm just so happy for you both. We always knew how much Genevieve loved you, and to see you both making each other very happy and starting a family, well, what is there not to cry about?"

Genevieve chuckled, and they sat just as a footman entered, carrying a tray of tea, afternoon cake, and biscuits.

"I adore her too, so the feeling is mutual. We'll be returning to my country estate at the end of the Season, so you will get to enjoy having our company until then. Maybe I could introduce you to a gentleman friend or two. Find you a husband as well."

Charlotte laughed and poured them both a cup of tea. "Thank you, but no, I shall be perfectly capable of finding my own husband."

Just then, the sound of a gentleman's voice burst into the drawing room, and Charlotte stood, a look of surprised delight crossing her features before she schooled them.

"Oh, I do beg your pardon, Lady Charlotte. I did not know you were occupying the room. I shall return later when you're finished here."

"Mr. Alexander Richards," Beckett said,

standing and going to the man whom Genevieve could not stop staring at. What a handsome gentleman, and who was he? And why was he barging into Lady Charlotte's drawing room?

She looked to her friend but found Charlotte staring at the man as well, her gaze one of awe and adoration.

Interesting...

"Lord Tyndall, good afternoon. It's good to see you again. It has been some time."

"Yes, it has. Years, in fact. What are you doing here?"

Mr. Richards glanced at Lady Charlotte and clasped his hands before him. "I'm Duke D'Estel's steward."

"By God, are you, man? Well, that's good for you, and if anyone knows their way around finances, it is you. It is good to see you again. We've missed you at the gambling dens. You always keep the players at their best."

"Ah, well, yes. But I rarely gamble these days."

Beckett laughed. "A good plan." He returned to sit beside Genevieve and Charlotte remained standing, staring at Mr. Richards as he stared back at her friend.

What was happening here that she did not know of?

"Well, I shall leave you to your tea."

"You may join us if you like, Mr. Richards. You're most welcome," Charlotte said, giving Mr. Richards the sweetest smile Genevieve had ever seen bestowed on anyone.

He cleared his throat but waved her words aside. "Alas, I must decline. Much to do. It was good to see you again, Lord Tyndall. Good afternoon, Lady Charlotte, Lady Tyndall."

He left them then, closing the door silently behind him. Genevieve met Charlotte's eyes, noting the blush that kissed her friend's pretty cheeks.

"What was that about?" she asked without hesitation.

Charlotte frowned, and attempted to appear confused. A total false economy because she knew her friend, and right now she was hiding something.

"I do not know what you mean," Charlotte answered innocently.

"Yes, you do. You like Mr. Richards, and he knows it. He could barely keep his eyes off you, either."

"Don't be absurd, Genevieve. You're so full of love these days that you see it where it does not exist elsewhere."

"That is not the case at all. You do like him,

and if I'm any judge of a man's desire, he likes you too."

Charlotte fought not to grin. "No, you are mistaken."

"Oh no, I'm not."

"You are, now enough about me. Tell me more about how you feel."

Genevieve let the line of questioning go, but she would eventually get it out of her. She glanced at Beckett, who grinned back, wiggling his brows before they started discussing the baby and their plans for the remainder of the Season.

But it was sure to be interesting, especially if her friend, a duke's daughter, was in lust with a steward.

Genevieve could not wait to see how that played out, hopefully with a happy ever after, as she had been gifted.

Charlotte deserved nothing less.

DON'T MISS TAMARA'S OTHER ROMANCE SERIES

Heiress

Diamond of the Season

Treasure of the Ton

Jewel of the Ball

1777 Society

One Night in London

Midnight in Mayfair

An Evening to Remember

Dalliance and Dukes

My Virtuous Duke

My Notorious Rogue

My Ruthless Beau

The Wayward Yorks

A Wager with a Duke

My Reformed Rogue

Wild, Wild, Duke

In the Duke of Time

Duke Around and Find Out

The Wayward Woodvilles

A Duke of a Time

On a Wild Duke Chase

Speak of the Duke

Every Duke has a Silver Lining

One Day my Duke Will Come

Surrender to the Duke

My Reckless Earl

Brazen Rogue

The Notorious Lord Sin

Wicked in My Bed

League of Unweddable Gentlemen

Tempt Me, Your Grace

Hellion at Heart

Dare to be Scandalous

To Be Wicked With You

Kiss Me, Duke

The Marquess is Mine

Kiss the Wallflower

A Midsummer Kiss

A Kiss at Mistletoe

A Kiss in Spring

To Fall For a Kiss

A Duke's Wild Kiss

To Kiss a Highland Rose

To Marry a Rogue

Only an Earl Will Do

Only a Duke Will Do

Only a Viscount Will Do

Only a Marquess Will Do

Only a Lady Will Do

Lords of London

To Bedevil a Duke

To Madden a Marquess

To Tempt an Earl

To Vex a Viscount

To Dare a Duchess

To Marry a Marchioness

Royal House of Atharia

To Dream of You

A Royal Proposition

Forever My Princess

A Time Traveler's Highland Love

To Conquer a Scot

To Save a Savage Scot

To Win a Highland Scot

A Stolen Season

A Stolen Season

A Stolen Season: Bath

A Stolen Season: London

Scandalous London

A Gentleman's Promise

A Captain's Order

A Marriage Made in Mayfair

High Seas & High Stakes

His Lady Smuggler

Her Gentleman Pirate

A Wallflower's Christmas Wreath

Daughters Of The Gods

Banished

Guardian

Fallen

Stand Alone Books

Defiant Surrender

A Brazen Agreement

To Sin with Scandal

Outlaws

ABOUT THE AUTHOR

Tamara is an Australian author who grew up in an old mining town in country South Australia, where her love of history was founded. So much so, she made her darling husband travel to the UK for their honeymoon, where she dragged him from one historical monument and castle to another.

A mother of three, her two little gentlemen in the making, a future lady (she hopes) keep her busy in the real world, but whenever she gets a moment's peace she loves to write romance novels in an array of genres, including regency, medieval and time travel.

Made in the USA
Columbia, SC
20 February 2025